D1570690

The Laws of Love

Lisa White

Best Wishes!

Lisa

CRIMSON
ROMANCE
Avon, Massachusetts

This edition published by
Crimson Romance
an imprint of F+W Media, Inc.
10151 Carver Road, Suite 200
Blue Ash, Ohio 45242

www.crimsonromance.com

Copyright © 2012 by Lisa Crockett White

ISBN 10: 1-4405-5230-4
ISBN 13: 978-1-4405-5230-4
eISBN 10: 1-4405-5229-0
eISBN 13: 978-1-4405-5229-8

Dedication

FOR MY HUSBAND, CHRIS

THE LOVE OF MY LIFE

Chapter One

Her stomach knotted with the day's growing frustration.

"Where is that wire?" Livi yelled into her assistant's office. "The money was supposed to be here two hours ago!" The young attorney walked out of her office and plopped down in the small leather office chair across from her assistant's desk. "Are we sure the fax went through? Did they get our signatures?"

"Yes. Calm down," her assistant Nadine said as she turned away from her computer to face her irritated boss. "They received our signatures, the contract is fully executed, and they have our correct wire instructions. Accounting simply hasn't received the money yet. Don't worry. It'll get here."

"I know the money will get here eventually, but I told Robert the deal would close *today*," Livi said, as if Nadine did not know that fact already.

Her assistant's calmness did nothing to improve Livi's mood. Last night's blind date fiasco had reminded Livi once again that her monogram's initials were not going to change anytime soon and thus she had started this morning off in a bad mood only to have the day plummet downhill from there. It had taken a year to negotiate this fifty million dollar deal and now it came down to a silly computer dictating when Hampton Steel's money would be received. Livi was not handling the delay well.

As Assistant General Counsel, Livi Miller had closed more deals for Hampton Steel Incorporated than she cared to remember and waiting for the other company to wire the money into her company's account had always been the most aggravating part of these transactions. In this age of technology, Livi did not understand why the wire could not be here with a simple press of a button. However, transferring money from one multi-million dollar corporation to another was not easy, and the layers of approvals between corporations and banks had gotten thicker in recent years thanks to Wall Street's ethical shortcomings.

In her head, David Bowie and Freddie Mercury were loudly and repeatedly singing "Under Pressure." She needed this deal to close today. While her job did not depend on it, she wanted everything to run smoothly right now. With her boss, Robert, retiring soon, Livi was next in line to take his place as general counsel. It was not official but Robert had implied Livi's succession so many times that the entire company assumed she would get the job.

Despite her boss's implications, however, Livi still questioned the absolute certainty of her promotion. Robert's drinking had reached a point where his legal opinions bordered on malpractice thus intensifying Hampton Steel's need for his retirement to occur sooner rather than later. While Livi could usually cover for her boss and his alcohol-influenced legal opinions, her promotion was entirely in his hands. Having her deal close today would reinforce Livi's ability as the company's top lawyer and hopefully cement her succession in the sometimes cloudy mind of her boss.

Thinking of this deal's impact on her promotion prompted Livi to grab a hefty handful of M&Ms from the crystal bowl sitting on the corner of Nadine's desk.

"Are you that worried?" her assistant asked.

"No." Livi smiled. "But I appreciate you keeping this stash for me." Chocolate had always been her "go-to" vice whenever she was anxious.

Livi had known Nadine since high school. They had not been best friends at Millersville High—Nadine had been the social butterfly while Livi stuck with her boyfriend and the school library. But when Livi was hired by Hampton Steel a few years ago, she was pleasantly surprised to find Nadine's familiar face in the assistant's chair outside her new office, and they had worked together as a team ever since. Livi appreciated having an old high school acquaintance around and was always careful to call Nadine her "assistant" and not "secretary". She knew how valuable Nadine was to her and did not want to point out the obvious working hierarchy between them.

"Would you please call accounting and check again?" Livi sighed as she walked back into her office while finishing off her M&Ms and gulping her third Diet Coke of the afternoon. She did not care that the caffeine could intensify her soon-to-be-here migraine. She just knew it made her feel better now. She would worry about the migraine once it got here tonight.

Livi sat down at her desk and stared out her office window, irritated with both her failed blind date and the delay in today's deal closing. She knew she loved her job, but stressful times like these caused Livi to question why she had not just married right out of high school and taken a simpler and more traditional path for her life as most of her friends had. However, Livi had been anything but traditional growing up and this nonconformity allowed her to discover her life's goal in the law as early as junior high school.

She had just completed seventh grade and was volunteering as a summer tour guide for Millersville's historic courthouse. While other kids her age were riding bikes along rural trails or swimming the cool waters of the local lake and river, Livi intently watched Millersville's petty legal dramas unfold from the back row of the courtroom. The law excited the geek in her and she absorbed it with the intensity of someone twice her age.

As she grew older, nothing could extinguish her excitement, so it was a natural progression for Livi to eventually leave her hometown of Millersville for college and law school. The University of Virginia had not been easy. Its reputation had been right on the mark. But while she questioned her chosen career path at times, she never regretted it, despite the constant reminders of what she was missing in her social life.

"Liv," Nadine called from her outer office. "Your dad is on line one."

Livi immediately realized she had forgotten tonight's birthday dinner for her sister. "Hey, Dad," Livi tried to sound nonchalant over the phone. "What time is dinner?"

"You know darn well dinner's at six o'clock. That time hasn't changed since I left you all those messages on your cell, and at home, and at work," her dad sweetly bristled. "Don't ask me what time dinner is and don't be late. Elizabeth is looking forward to spending time with you and I know you can stop working long enough to celebrate her birthday."

Livi sighed. "Don't worry. I just have one more thing to close out and I'll be there with bells on."

"Well, I don't care what you're wearing. Just make sure you bring your undivided attention. And Livi. . ." Her dad paused.

"Yes, Dad," she said, anxious to get off the phone.

"I love you."

"I know, Dad. Love you too." Livi hung up the phone. "Nadine!" Livi called into her assistant's office. "What did accounting say?"

Nadine was already standing in Livi's doorway, her arms crossed and eyebrows raised in an I-told-you-so fashion. "You forgot your sister's birthday dinner, didn't you?" she said, ignoring Livi's question.

"Yes," Livi rolled her eyes.

"Well, today must be your lucky day," Nadine smiled. "Accounting just received the wire so the deal has officially closed. You now have time to go downtown and get your sister something she actually wants—not whatever you can grab on the way like you usually do. So why don't you get out of here?"

With her multi-million dollar deal closed, Livi took a deep breath and finally relaxed. "Shopping is my thing." She beamed with an immediate mood change as she began packing up her briefcase. "Call me on my cell if anything comes up," she yelled to Nadine who had already retreated back to her office.

"I always do," said Nadine as she sat down in front of her computer again. "I'm just shocked you're actually leaving the office on time."

"Chalk it up to family guilt," Livi joked as she headed out the door.

*

Livi parked near her favorite store but decided to walk around downtown Millersville before hitting her beloved antique shop. A fall breeze helped push her along as she strolled, and while most of the trees had not yet reached their full color potential, Livi was already keyed up for the season to come. Fall was her favorite time of year, and she especially loved a Millersville fall. Set in the mountains of Virginia, Millersville was founded in the late 1800s by Livi's great-great grandfather, James Bradford Miller.

The town began as the only railway stop for miles, but GranPa Miller, as he was known, had positioned the town on the map when he established the first department store in the area. Even though any money her ancestors had was long gone, and Miller's Department Store closed in the 1960s, the Miller name was still prevalent throughout the area as evidenced by the faded paint on several downtown buildings. The Miller and Sons Dry Goods building now housed the local pub and Miller First National Bank had been remodeled into Nell's, Livi's favorite antique store.

In more recent years, a downtown resurgence had produced new, unique shops and restaurants, once again positioning Millersville as *the* place to be in the region. The town spent thousands of dollars on new sidewalks, lighting and landscaping in the downtown area, and today's busy streets were evidence of a successful investment. Tax breaks were granted to businesses that moved into town, and, thus, Hampton Steel, Livi's employer, made the astute decision to relocate its headquarters in Millersville.

These tax breaks, combined with the local non-union workforce, had helped the company become Millersville's primary employer as well as one of the top steel fabricating plants in the country. Hampton Steel's move also provided Livi the opportunity to practice what her father called "big city" corporate law while maintaining her hometown roots.

Olivia Grace "Livi" Miller was born and raised in Millersville and she loved everything about it. Familiarity of sidewalk smells and the knowledge that she recognized almost everyone in town gave her a comfort level living here on her own. Livi was fascinated with her hometown's history, and she had recently lucked into buying a home in the older, established section of town just blocks from where she was now walking. The home was not large, but it was not a cottage either and had enough room for her and her large mutt, Gatsby, to have their own space when needed. It had been built by some long-forgotten ancestor of Livi's and, overall, was still in fairly good shape. She was slowly filling it with the English antiques she loved and hoped to have her dining room complete in time to host her family's Christmas dinner.

After browsing a few of the other downtown stores, Livi finally found herself at Nell's. With her limited free time spent decorating, the antique store had become her new home away from home. She took a deep breath as she walked into the store and immediately began to forget today's stresses. She knew she would leave Nell's with more shopping bags than she needed, filled with more items for herself than for her sister.

The bank building's smell still permeated the shop's plastered walls and the dark hardwood floors creaked with history. Bank teller windows had been uniquely converted to display cases showcasing Nell's latest acquisitions from her contacts in the antiques world, and upon a quick review of today's displays, Livi immediately saw something she wanted for herself. There, propped up in the center teller window, was the most gorgeous Imari platter she had ever seen. The blue and orange details intricately woven on the large porcelain oval popped out at her screaming, *Take me home*—or so Livi envisioned until a little voice from the back of her head whispered, *Remember your sister.*

With one quick look at the price tag and a small choke as she realized her checkbook would not allow her this luxury right now, Livi began browsing for her sister's gift. The antique platter's perfect spot on her dining room wall would remain empty for now.

"I saw your heart flutter at that one." Nell Cooper Harris laughed as she came out of the back storeroom wiping sweat off her brow and hair out of her eyes with hands gloved in a workman's dirty suede. "I just got that in from Atlanta."

"Well, my heart may be fluttering but if I don't get Elizabeth's birthday present before six o'clock tonight, my butt will be burning with my dad's boot print. By the way, you look a mess," Livi joked as she headed to the next display case.

"Inventory." Nell sighed and smiled. "Did you have anything in mind?"

"No. You know Elizabeth. She's hard to buy for. She flits from one interest to another so it's hard to know what this week's passion is." Livi loved her younger sister but her own Type A personality never understood Elizabeth's artsy side.

Nell walked over to Livi and gave her the usual welcoming hug. "I think I might have just the thing for our Elizabeth," she said, motioning for Livi to follow her.

Like Livi, Nell had grown up in Millersville and moved away for college, but after graduating with a degree in art history, she and her college sweetheart had settled back into her familiar Millersville life. Nell's husband, Richard, was an entry-level bookkeeper at Hampton Steel, so Livi saw at least one of them almost every day and considered the couple two of her closest friends. Nell appeared to effectively balance her sole proprietor image with that of soccer mom to her three children, and, at times, Livi envied her. Nell had succeeded with the two-sided life Livi envisioned for herself, maintaining a career on one side and a family on the other. But being raised Baptist in a small southern town meant that before Livi could check "having children" off her Life List, she needed to check off "find true love and get married." So, while she had maintained control of the career side of her life, Livi had been unable to find the socially acceptable order of her life's personal side. Nevertheless, whenever she felt her envy of

Nell creeping back in, Livi rationalized to herself that Nell was a few years older and had had more time to develop her perfect life. Livi liked to believe she still had a few more years for her Life List to establish its own proper order.

"What about this?" Nell said, holding up an antique brooch enameled in candy-apple red—an appropriate gift for an elementary school teacher.

"Perfect." Livi smiled.

As Nell wrapped the gift at the front counter, Livi's eyes glanced at the framed photo hanging over the cash register. It never failed. Every time she stood at that counter, her heart beat faster as she tried not to look at his green eyes. The photo showed Nell's younger brother, Jake, dressed in his desert camouflage posing with his friend, Ben, both grinning from ear to ear despite their obvious surroundings. The dust on Jake's face made the green of his eyes more intense and, although the photo appeared to be somewhat recent, Livi thought Jake's eyes looked just as they did in high school.

The military and rugged sands of Iraq had not dimmed the sparkle and mischief radiating from those eyes, and they still revealed an old soul that held a special place in Livi's heart. Today especially, with the barrage of reminders of what Livi's life lacked, these green eyes attacked Livi's heart more than usual and she allowed herself to wander through her minefield of memories while she waited on Elizabeth's gift to be wrapped.

By all accounts, Jake Cooper was Livi's first love, and except for a mistaken stint with a fellow law student that truly did not count, Livi probably considered Jake her only love. All of Livi's other beaus had been measured by her "Jake" standard and, unfortunately for them, none had ever reached Jake's level in Livi's heart. They began dating at the end of their sophomore year of high school, and the following summer taught Livi the joys of young, carefree love with a boy who admired her as much as he adored her. They spent that summer swimming in the lake, hiking the local hills and learning how to hold hands in a way that made Livi's heart take precedence over her mind's legal ambitions. Over time, Jake taught her to fly-fish and she taught him which fork to use with shrimp at her graduation dinner. For their senior prom, they even learned to dance the shag together just like Livi's parents used to dance on the Myrtle Beach boardwalk in their younger days.

The two teenagers made a beautiful couple. Livi had long, dark hair and "girl-next-door" looks. Jake was ruggedly handsome with his green eyes and tall, broad build. His obvious strength contrasted with the sweetness he showered on Livi, and her blue eyes melted whenever he gave her that special look. Their relationship was the envy of the high school gossip mill, for they met the clichéd definition of opposites attract. He was star player of the football team. She was star member of the debate team. While Jake spent his afternoons in the gym, Livi spent her time in the library. However, for whatever reason, when they were together it was as if heaven had thrown a star around the two of them and each one glowed brighter than when they were apart. The laughter they accumulated over the two and a half years they dated was immeasurable, and Livi's memories of their time together had become more romanticized in recent years, pushing aside the realities of why their time together had ended.

When all was said and done, Livi blamed herself for their break up. The summer after their high school graduation had been a confusing mix of plans and memories. Both fully intended to stay together but each knew that fall was closing in on them. As summer ended and Livi packed her bags for Charlottesville, she and Jake told each other that distance would not affect what they had.

However, time had different intentions and, while they tried to keep in touch, the calls and visits became fewer and fewer. Livi worked to maintain her grades and Jake searched for his lot in life assuming Livi was quickly leaving him behind. By the time her exams were over that first semester and she returned home for Christmas, Jake had already left for California with Ben. He had told her that he had a line on a great job but that he had to be out west before the first of December. Thus, Livi came home to an empty holiday realizing she and Jake had broken up without either really saying the words.

Deciding to ask the question that had never been asked in all her time spent in Nell's store, Livi's remembrances forced her to blurt out, "So, how's Jake?"

Nell stopped wrapping the gift and looked up with a grin that competed with the Cheshire Cat's. "Do you have ESP or something?" she said.

"No." Livi was confused.

"Then why don't you ask him yourself?" Nell loudly called out, "Jake!"

And with that one word, Livi turned to see her past rounding the corner out of the back storeroom and looking better than anything she had seen in quite a while.

Chapter Two

Livi braced herself against the front counter, instinctively sucking in her stomach and wishing she had not eaten that last handful of M&Ms at the office. She had not seen Jake in over ten years and her self-conscious vanity suddenly exploded to the surface. *Why did I not wear my black pantsuit today?* Livi thought as she manipulated her jacket around in order to cover her waistline.

"Hey, Liv." Jake strode toward her and gave her a quick-release hug.

His strong arms felt good around her and their bodies briefly pressed together without intention. Could he actually feel her nauseous stomach turning somersaults? "Hey, stranger. Long time no see. I had no idea you were back in town." *Just act natural,* Livi thought as she reached behind her back for the much-needed counter again.

"Yeah. Just got back in town a few days ago. Nell's kept me under wraps and pretty busy. You would think she was paying me with the hours I've been working."

"I've fed you, haven't I?" Nell retorted from behind the counter.

"Yep, that's me. Will work for food." Jake still had his mischievous grin.

"So how have you been?" Livi was trying to be cordial even if her stomach was now beyond nauseous and tying itself in knots again. She noticed Nell place the wrapped gift on the counter and discretely slide into the back storeroom. *Please don't leave me alone with him*, she thought as she watched the storeroom door close.

"I've been good." Jake smiled. "Got out of the service last spring and have been traveling around ever since. I finally decided I needed some time at home so Millersville is my latest stop. How about you? Still working the long hours at Hampton Steel?"

"Unfortunately, yes. Those student loans won't go away on their own. But since most of the town seems to work there, I still get to see some old friends every now and then. Do you remember Nadine Wilcox?" Livi's head was now officially spinning and she clutched the counter even tighter.

"Sure. Blonde, very social?" Jake's eyes were smiling.

"Yeah. That's her. She's my administrative assistant now. Hasn't changed much. Still the social butterfly. But she makes the office fun." Livi loved looking into his green eyes. *Keep it together*, she thought to herself as she nervously continued, "Uh, . . .Nell has kept me up on your parents. I know they're glad you're home."

"Yeah, they're great. Dad still gets up at the crack of dawn and Mom spends her time helping with Nell's kids. They're enjoying being grandparents. Mom's been cooking up a storm since I got home. Between her and Nell, I've probably gained ten pounds in the past few days." Jake patted his obviously still hard stomach. "So, how's your dad?"

Livi had to forcibly avert her eyes away from Jake's abs as she answered, "He's fine. Still set in his ways. Elizabeth moved back to town so he has both of us to bug now. He's retired and spends most of his time on the river fly-fishing. I'm on my way to his house tonight for Elizabeth's birthday dinner." Livi glanced at the gift on the counter. Is he going to admit this is awkward or are they really going to continue with this question and answer period normally reserved for game show hosts and their guests?

"Please tell her I said happy birthday. I still think of her as the little kid that used to sneak up on us while we were making out on your parents' couch."

And there it was. With that one comment, the memories of his kisses combined with the somersaulting M&Ms in her knotted stomach, and Livi thought she would throw up all over Jake's plaid flannel shirt. "Well. . .I better get going. I promised Dad I would be on time for once. It was so good seeing you. How. . .uh. . . how long are you in town?" Livi was trying to be polite but she just had to get out of there. She grabbed the gift and started backing toward the door as she felt her stomach tighten even more.

"I'm not on a schedule so far. I promised my dad I would help fix up the guest house and bring it into the twenty-first century so I may be here for a while," Jake said in an obvious attempt to be funny, but Livi could not think of anything but getting out of there.

"Well, uh. . .take care. It was good seeing you. Please thank Nell for her help with Elizabeth's gift," Livi said as she turned to rush out the door.

*

Jake watched her walk out with that same sway she had in high school. With Livi's notorious work schedule, Jake had not expected to run into her while he was in town, but seeing her sway as she walked to her car conjured up unexpected memories that made him thankful for their impromptu meeting. He stood there a long time looking out the store window until she was finally in her car and driving off. He smiled a little, experiencing a faint but familiar warm feeling inside, then he headed back to the storeroom.

*

Livi could not get her car door open fast enough. Under her breath, she chastised herself for parking directly in front of the store. She knew Jake could see her every move as she got into her car and prayed it would start quickly. Her old BMW had been stalling lately, and she really needed it to work this time if she were to make her grand exit. Luckily, the ignition did not disappoint her, and Livi drove off making sure the store disappeared quickly in her rearview mirror.

Her body was still in shock from Jake's hug, her mind was reeling from looking into his eyes. Her old beau had not changed. Maybe he had a few more lines around his eyes, but he did not look older, just wiser. A few chest hairs now peeked through the top of his flannel shirt but his body still moved like a teenager. *Man, he looked good*, she thought as memories continued to flood her brain like a tsunami.

With her thoughts swirling, Livi was fortunate her destination was familiar, and her car seemed to drive itself to her father's subdivision. Mr. Miller still lived in the home where she grew up and nothing about the neighborhood had changed in thirty years. It was established before the historical fixer-upper fad of the 1990s, when *Knots Landing* subdivisions were en vogue.

The neighborhood had been the hot place for the middle class to settle down in Millersville, where a budding architect could keep his wife and two daughters safe and conventional. Their life had been comfortable but not opulent, simple but not boring, and their neighbors' lives had been identical. The entire subdivision and its inhabitants had grown old together with routines that did not change despite the town's growth. Livi experienced déjà-vu as she drove through the neighborhood entrance while still feeling Jake's arms around her. It was as if she were back in high school.

As she neared her father's house, Livi spotted her sister's Jeep already parked in the driveway and she decided not to mention seeing Jake to her family. They had all loved Jake and she knew they secretly blamed Livi's ambition for his departure from their lives. She parked behind the Jeep and sat in her car until her stomach calmed down and she once again felt in control. Livi then left her car's quietness and carried Elizabeth's gift along the well-known brick path to her father's front door. She entered without knocking as she always did, still rightfully feeling this was her home.

Being in her childhood home immediately calmed Livi even more and the stress of her day was left on the front doorstep as she felt her mother's warmth envelop her through the home's old paint and furnishings. Livi's mother had been an antique lover also and the home still exuded Mrs. Miller's well-known charm. Her maternal presence in the home was still evident despite the fact Mrs. Miller had not physically lived there for many years and Livi was grateful her father had no plans to redecorate.

Smelling the pungent garlic and tomato aroma of her dad's spaghetti, she heard her father and sister back in the kitchen bantering over basil amounts. Livi continued to compose herself as she walked down the hall to the kitchen. She then took a deep breath and rounded the corner with her arms in the air and shouted, "Ta-duh!"

"Livi! I knew you'd make it!" Elizabeth squealed as she ran to Livi whose arms dropped down to give the birthday girl a hug as only a big sister could.

"Well, will wonders never cease? There she is without her briefcase. What happened? Did you get fired?" Mr. Miller teased.

"Funny, Dad," Livi placed the gift on the kitchen counter. "What can I do to help?"

"Tell Dad the sauce needs more basil," Elizabeth remarked as she went to the stove and stirred the pot.

"You should know by now that Dad's sauce is perfect every time. I wouldn't mess with his recipe if my life depended on it," Livi said as she kissed her father's cheek and began setting the kitchen table. Although it had been years, it was still hard for Livi to skip over her mother's chair at these family dinners. The car wreck had been ruled an accident but its result was so immediate that Livi never had a chance to say good-bye. Mrs. Miller's death had left a hole in Livi's heart that would never be filled but, in the end, the tragedy had helped her become a better lawyer.

Losing Jake in college and her mother's sudden death during law school had boosted Livi's work ethic. Work became something she could usually control. She had thrown herself in the law and pushed her sadness to the back of her heart, concreting her workaholic reputation.

"Dinner's ready but we'll wait on Todd to eat," Mr. Miller said as he grabbed a Coors Light from the refrigerator while Elizabeth opened a bottle of Beaulieu Pinot Noir. Knowing Todd, Elizabeth's boyfriend, would have a beer with her father, Livi only grabbed two wine glasses from the cabinet, for herself and her sister.

"Cheers," Elizabeth said after she halfway filled the two glasses. "So how is work?"

"Fine." Livi's standard answer to the standard question. She did not have anything else going on in her life so that was all people knew to ask. Before they each could take their second sip of wine, Todd, bounded in the back door.

"There's my birthday girl!" Todd grabbed Elizabeth with a hug and twirled her around. They had only been dating for four months, but Todd was a Millersville child also and had known their family forever. He was younger than Livi but older than Elizabeth and had graduated from the same high school.

"*Now* we can finally eat," said Mr. Miller as he started mounding the spaghetti on the plates. Elizabeth grabbed a beer for Todd and they all took their pre-appointed seats at the table. Even Todd knew not to sit in Mrs. Miller's chair. It always remained empty at these family functions and was a reminder she was missed.

"Todd, why don't you say the blessing," Mr. Miller said, establishing the dinner's proper order, and they all bowed their heads. Livi loved these traditional mementos of why the world turned round. Todd's prayer ended with an "Amen" in unison.

"So, Livi, what's up in the big corporate world?" Todd's version of the standard question.

"Not much. I'd rather hear about your job," Livi intentionally changed the subject. "Did you put anyone we know in jail this week?" Todd was a deputy for the local sheriff's department and always had stories of someone they knew participating in Millersville's weekly Saturday night scuffles.

"Not this week. Last Friday's football game was interesting with a few teenagers marking their territory—but no big deal," Todd responded as he lovingly looked over at Elizabeth and smiled. They were a cute, young, happy couple who did not appear to have a care in the world. Elizabeth's teaching schedule and his schedule as deputy allowed them to spend a lot of time together, and a marriage proposal was assumed in the near future. Both Livi and her father liked them together and were glad Elizabeth had finally picked someone worthy of her.

The young couple complimented each other with Todd grounding her flighty side and Elizabeth lessening his serious side. Already Todd acted and felt like a member of the Miller family and had no problem taking a long swig of beer at Mr. Miller's dinner table. "Hey, you'll never guess who I saw this morning at the bagel shop," Todd said, setting his beer back down on the table.

"Who?" Mr. Miller said as he passed the bread basket to Livi.

"Jake Cooper. He's back in town for a while staying with his parents."

As if on cue, Livi accidentally dropped the bread basket and its contents on the floor. She had really wanted to avoid this topic of conversation. Mr. Miller and Elizabeth gave each other a knowing look and they both started laughing.

"Obviously news to Livi," Elizabeth said as she rolled her eyes toward the bread basket on the floor.

"Actually, no, it's not news to me. I ran into Jake this afternoon at Nell's." Picking up the bread off the floor, Livi regained her composure. "He's just in town for a visit."

"Did he ask you out?" Elizabeth jumped the gun.

"No. What are you talking about? We haven't seen each other in years but you automatically assume we still have the hots for each other." Suddenly Livi was on the defensive.

"Well, would you go out with him if he asked?" Elizabeth would not let it go.

"Elizabeth, change the subject." Livi looked over at her father and pleaded, "Dad, tell her to cut it out."

Mr. Miller enjoyed their exchange and was reminded that sisters never change. "Leave your sister alone, Elizabeth," Mr. Miller instructed as he took a large swig of his own beer. He then turned to Livi and said matter-of-factly, "Livi, answer your sister's question."

"Dad! None of your business," Livi bristled. She was getting aggravated.

Ignoring Livi's irritation, Mr. Miller replied, "Well, would you go out with him? Work isn't a life, you know. You could stand a little down time, and I remember you and Jake had a lot of fun together. You don't have to marry the guy. Just do something other than work for a change." Mr. Miller secretly worried Livi would end up with nothing but a bank account and the proverbial retirement watch if she continued with her career-only attitude.

"Everyone lay off," Livi said firmly. "I am fine. Besides, he wouldn't be interested in me. We are in two different places now. I live and work here. He is just passing through. No need to pretend we are still in high school." Deep down, Livi did not want to believe what she was saying, but she was not about to let them know how her stomach and its contents had turned somersaults this afternoon when she saw Jake.

"I'm sorry I mentioned him," said Todd.

The remaining dinner conversation purposefully avoided the topic of Jake and instead centered on Elizabeth's birthday, her school children's antics and Mr. Miller's latest catch while fly-fishing the local river. Moving to the home's back deck for birthday cake and coffee, the four watched the sunset while the conversation turned to local politics and gossip. The phone rang in the kitchen as Elizabeth was opening her gift from Livi.

"I'll get it." Mr. Miller headed into the house.

"Oh, Livi! I love it." Elizabeth stood up to model the brooch now pinned on her jacket.

"I found it at Nell's and thought it looked like you." Livi was pleased with herself for choosing the perfect gift for Elizabeth's current tastes.

"Was that before or after you saw Jake?" Elizabeth said.

"Elizabeth, I said let it go." Livi did not want to get into it again.

"I know what you said. But, you were just so happy with him. I'd like it if you all were back together. That's all," Elizabeth said seriously. Todd sat in silence, knowing this was a sister talk to which he was not invited.

"I appreciate you being concerned with my happiness. But I really meant it when I said we are in two different places now. He's traveling and this is just his latest stop on his way to who knows where. I, on the other hand, am embedded here. I enjoy my work and, with my boss retiring soon, I may be moving up the Hampton Steel ladder faster than I ever expected. I probably won't have time for anything else for a while." Livi smiled at her sister and patted her hand. "Look, I know you mean well, but Jake and I are just heading in separate directions. Please be understanding about this."

"Okay, "Elizabeth relented. "I just want you to be as happy as I am." Elizabeth leaned over and gave Todd a kiss on the cheek. "It's not so bad being in love, you know," she said to Livi while gazing into Todd's eyes.

"Look, I'll let you two handle the love in our family and I'll stick to work. Besides, Jake's as uninterested as I am in starting back up again," Livi tried to convince herself.

"Liv! Phone." Mr. Miller called from the kitchen.

"Me?" Livi was puzzled. Who would be calling her at her father's house? Did Hampton Steel implant a tracking device in her without her knowing?

"Yes, you." Her dad leaned through the back door. "It's Jake."

Chapter Three

The silence on the back porch was awkward. Todd and Elizabeth stared at Livi, Livi stared at her father, and her father just stood in the doorway, grinning. There went Livi's stomach again.

"Well, I said come get the phone," Mr. Miller commanded, still grinning.

Livi did not say a word as she took the cordless phone from her father and crossed through the kitchen into the formal dining room for some privacy. She glanced back to see her father close the door behind him and deliberately block Elizabeth from following her.

In the home's formal dining room with Mrs. Miller's antique china collection covering the calming Wedgwood blue walls, Livi closed her eyes and took a deep breath. "Hello," she cautiously said into the phone.

"Hey, Liv." Jake sounded casual.

"Hey. I've talked to you more today than in the past ten years." Livi again tried to sound nonchalant as she sat down in one of her mother's antique Queen Anne dining chairs, her stomach still quietly somersaulting.

"Yeah. It was good seeing you today. I was just thinking, you, uh, haven't been out to the farm in a while and, uh, I thought you might want to see what I'm doing to the guesthouse."

Does Jake sound nervous? Livi thought. "Uh, yeah. That would be fine," she said.

"Okay. I hear your schedule is crazy but would tomorrow after work be good with you?" said Jake.

"Sure," said Livi, not knowing what else to say.

"Nell showed me where you live. Could I pick you up at five-thirty or is that too early? Are you off work by then?"

No, not usually, thought Livi. Today was the first time in a long time she had left her office before eight o'clock at night. "Five-thirty sounds good," she lied.

"Great. See you then. If anything changes, just call Nell's. I'll be there all day tomorrow."

"Okay. See you tomorrow." Livi hung up the phone wondering what just happened. She has not seen this guy in years and the next thing she knows she has a date with him tomorrow. *Wait, is it a date?* thought Livi, *Or is Jake just looking for an old friend to hang out with?*

Well, whatever the reason, Livi had plans to see Jake tomorrow night and she was good with that. It would be nice spending time with an old friend she hadn't seen in a while. Putting up her defenses, Livi immediately began rationalizing their upcoming meeting as anything but romantic. She returned to the back porch where all eyes were on her.

"Well?" Elizabeth pounced. She could not stand the suspense thickly hanging over the back deck.

"I'm going to visit his parents' farm after work tomorrow," Livi said casually.

"He asked you out on a date?"

"No. It's not a date. We're just two old friends getting together for a visit. He wants to show me the guesthouse he is fixing up." Livi tried to sound convincing.

"Ok. Whatever you say. But I still think it is a date." With neither side conceding, this conversation topic ended with Elizabeth getting in the last word and Livi feigning indifference.

*

The next day, Livi woke up with a new feeling in her stomach. Thankfully, it was not the nauseating somersaults from the day before. Instead, today she felt butterflies. *Wow, I haven't felt those in a while*, Livi thought as she stretched out in her bed. Livi's butterflies had been missing from her life for a long time and her career had slowly, but reluctantly, taken their place. Sure, she got excited about closing a deal at work or finding just the right chair to accompany her antique desk at home. But this type of excitement was grounded in material, or goal-oriented, logic. Livi's butterflies were different. Her butterflies were far from logical and their only goal was to shove emotion right smack dab into the middle of her one-sided, career-oriented life. Livi knew that, in the past, her emotions had been tied to a particular person—her mother, her father, Jake—so feeling her butterflies this morning was an indication that someone had invaded her emotions.

This thought bothered her because she did not have time for her emotions or her butterflies right now. She needed to concentrate on work and her upcoming promotion. Nevertheless, past experiences had taught Livi that her butterflies could not be trained into submission and so she reluctantly resigned herself to spending the rest of her day in a no-win struggle to keep her butterflies under control.

As she got dressed for work that morning, Livi's subconscious forced her to take an extra long shower and to apply her make-up with more attention to detail than she had in a while. While her mind kept asserting tonight's meeting with Jake was not a date, her heart disagreed. Always the professional, she tried not to let this internal struggle affect her tasks at work and so, outwardly, Livi spent the day going through her usual work routine with her coworkers.

She even tried to meet up with her boss to review yesterday's deal closing but he had someone in his office. Livi did not recognize the man, and her boss's assistant was less than helpful when Livi asked about him. The heavy wooden door to the general counsel's office was open so she could see both her boss and the stranger. The stranger was dressed in what she thought was an Armani suit but Livi could not see his shoes. While the man and his suit looked very polished, Livi thought you could always tell more about a man by his shoes so she reserved her opinion of the stranger until she could see his feet.

Ordinarily, curiosity would have forced her to wait outside the general counsel's office so that she could eventually opine on the stranger's feet, but today, thoughts of Jake and tonight's meeting overrode any curiosity she had and she quickly returned to her office without determining the status of the man's shoes.

"You seem distracted today," said Nadine as Livi walked past her assistant's desk.

"No. Just tired from yesterday." Livi did not want anyone else to know about tonight, especially Nadine. Her assistant was very talkative, and Livi did not want everyone thinking she had a date with Jake if Jake had other intentions.

The day passed quickly with Livi wanting to leave the office by four-thirty that afternoon. She knew if she gave herself that goal, she would have a chance of getting out of there by five o'clock. She started packing her briefcase at four thirty-five, surprising Nadine with her early departure.

"See you tomorrow," Livi said over her shoulder as she headed toward the door.

"Are you sick?" Nadine was utterly confused.

"No. Like I said, just tired." Livi exited without giving her assistant a chance to respond. Her butterflies returned on her short drive home, but she again told herself there would be no romance tonight. She parked in her driveway and quickly ran the few steps to her front door.

Gatsby greeted her inside but also seemed puzzled by her early arrival home. She stopped to give the dog his routine hug, which had the intended result of putting him at ease and he settled back into his bed by the living room fireplace. A quick glance around the room and Livi mentally marked "clean living room" off of her list of things to do before Jake arrived. Being a workaholic meant there was never anyone home to make a mess so the living room was in the clear. Livi raced back to her bedroom assuming Jake's notorious punctuality had only gotten worse with his years in the military. She knew he would be here precisely at five-thirty and she wanted to be ready.

During a boring meeting with a group of coworkers earlier this afternoon, she had finally decided what she would wear tonight so that she could quickly attack her closet when she arrived home. She rarely wore blue jeans but they seemed appropriate for visiting Jake's farm, so she pulled out the only pair she could find from the back of her closet.

After changing into her chosen outfit, she thoroughly checked herself in the mirror and determined she could not tuck in her designated white, button-down shirt tonight without her butt being the center of attention. Livi realized she really needed to get back into her workout routine if she was going to wear these jeans again. After a hurried review of her closet, she quickly changed out of the shirt and into a brown, V-neck sweater that partially covered her rear but made her breasts appear bigger, thereby balancing out her backside. After pulling on her old cowboy boots, she flounced her long, dark hair, touched up her make-up and realized she had time for a quick glass of wine before Jake arrived.

That would definitely settle her butterflies. She poured herself a glass of merlot and sat on the living room sofa with Gatsby settling in beside her. The wine helped Livi decide that her nervousness was unnecessary. Tonight was simply a meeting between friends. They would laugh at old times. They would catch up. This was not going anywhere. Jake was just in town for a while, and she had way too much going on at work to deal with a guy right now. By the time she finished her wine, Livi had convinced herself that tonight was nothing and she had no feelings for Jake other than as an old friend. Her butterflies had officially flown away.

Gatsby heard something outside and clumsily ran to the front door. Despite this attentiveness, he really was not much of a watchdog. He never barked. He never growled. He usually just stood at the door wagging his stubby tail waiting for his obligatory attention. He greeted everyone the same, strangers and friends alike. He considered them all potential head rubs so Gatsby never discriminated.

Livi peeked out the window and saw a white Chevy pickup truck parked on the street in front of her house and assumed it was Jake's. If it had been a Ford, she might have assumed differently, but Jake had always been a Chevy man, and it would have insulted him if she did not remember this fact. She stood up and took one last look at herself in her large foyer mirror just as Jake knocked at the door. *No big deal. This is no big deal*, she kept thinking over and over again. She took a deep breath and opened the door. There stood Jake in blue jeans, boots, an old, tan, L.L. Bean barn jacket, and the sexiest smile in the world.

No big deal, my ass, she thought. *The butterflies are back and they have multiplied ten-fold.*

Chapter Four

"Hey Liv. Ready to go?" Jake looked down and gave Gatsby the expected head rub. "Who's this?"

"Gatsby. He's my pound puppy I found a few years ago." Livi clutched her stomach as if trying to hold in her butterflies.

"Looks like he has some German Short-haired Pointer in him." Jake knew his hunting dogs. "I bet he's pretty smart."

"No. Pretty spoiled is more like it." Livi grabbed her casual coat, also an L.L. Bean barn jacket, just not nearly as worn as Jake's, and closed the front door with Gatsby whining on the other side.

"Do you want to take him with us?" asked Jake.

"No. He's fine. He's used to me leaving for work. He just knows how to play on your sympathies." Livi nervously laughed. Her butterflies had officially landed in full force and appeared to be settling in for the night.

Jake opened Livi's door and she pulled herself up into the truck. She watched Jake as he rounded the front of the pickup, a grin absolutely covering his chiseled face, and she again felt like she was back in high school. The ride out to his parents' farm was short and filled with nervous small talk, neither knowing exactly how to act now that they were adults.

It was there, in the cab of Jake's truck, that Livi felt fuller than she had felt in quite a while. Before that ride, she had assumed she was missing something, that her hectic career-oriented life was lopsided. But until that moment in Jake's truck, she had never really known exactly *what* it was she was missing. She had already resigned herself to living her one-sided life a long time ago, to maintaining a level of control, to living up to her reputation.

She had assumed her opportunity for a fuller life had passed and she was okay with that—at least that is what she had kept telling herself. But there, riding in Jake's truck, she finally felt like she had it all, even if it was only for tonight.

They soon crossed through the gated entrance to the Cooper farm and started down the long, oak-covered driveway. In the large, picturesque field adjacent to the driveway, horses played, enjoying the coolness of the evening, and, while the sun had not yet set, the sky was already beginning to turn the brilliant orange-yellow-red color that only the Virginia mountains could hold. Although the field's setting looked romantic, the nervousness that pervaded the silence of the truck's cab downplayed any such thoughts for either Jake or Livi and soon they were turning in front of the Cooper's large white farmhouse.

Jake stopped the truck abruptly and turned to Livi. "Do you mind if we go in for a minute? Mom and Dad said they wanted to see you if that's okay."

"Sure," said Livi. *So he told his parents about tonight*, she thought. Livi started to open her door and realized Jake was already at her side opening it for her. They walked to the front door in contented silence.

"Mom!" Jake called out as they entered the farmhouse foyer. It was an older farmhouse, built by Jake's grandfather. Like the Miller house, the Cooper home had not changed much over the years either. The only difference Livi could see was the addition of grandchildren's pictures, which absolutely covered the foyer and stairway walls. The wallpaper may have faded but the memories had not, and Livi felt unusually comfortable standing there waiting on Jake's parents. Mr. and Mrs. Cooper came out of the kitchen in the back, both smiling as they headed straight for Livi.

"Livi!" Jake's mother got to Livi first and wrapped her arms around her. "We are so glad you came out to visit! How about some coffee and cake?" A true southerner, Mrs. Cooper always thought food was the key to hospitality.

"Janelle, she just got here. Give her time to think." Mr. Cooper waved off Mrs. Cooper and looked down at Livi as he put an arm around her and asked, "How are you, sweetie?" His shirt smelled like his pipe, triggering more of Livi's memories. Her brain was in overdrive and her newly found butterflies were hyperactive beyond belief.

"I'm fine. Thank you." Livi smiled, again clutching her stomach in an attempt to quiet her newfound friends.

Jake stepped in. "You two act like you never see her. You all live in the same town, for Pete's sake."

"Well, we really don't see her that often and especially not for a visit in our home. Miss Livi is our local big time attorney and doesn't get out of her office that much." Mrs. Cooper knowingly smiled. "We are so proud of you!"

"Thank you." Livi did not know what to say at that. Was that a compliment or an implication that she worked too much?

"Well, sit, sit." Mrs. Cooper began to usher them into the front living room.

"Mom, we just stopped by for a minute. I want Livi to see the guesthouse before the sun sets," Jake said.

Sunset? With Jake? Livi thought. There went her butterflies again.

"Oh, all right." Mrs. Cooper turned to Livi. "Maybe next time we can visit longer. Jake has big plans to turn around that guesthouse so you really should see it."

They all four walked onto the large front porch with Livi promising Mrs. Cooper that she would definitely come back for coffee and cake another time. Once again, Jake opened her door and she climbed in the truck. They drove the short distance to the back of the property where the guesthouse sat along the river. It was built as a bunkhouse for the farm workers at the turn of the century and had experienced very few updates since then.

The Coopers had added a bathroom and updated the kitchen slightly but the other rooms remained untouched. When Jake was younger, the Coopers had hosted overnights for the local Boy Scouts and the large bedroom of the bunkhouse had been convenient to house his large troop. Later, in high school, Jake had hosted many a late night party here so Livi knew the old guesthouse well.

"Well, here we are." Jake said as they pulled up to the front door. "I haven't had time to do much so don't expect it to be finished."

"I'm sure Nell's inventory has been keeping you busy. Don't worry about my expectations," Livi responded. Her double meaning of the word *expectations* was intended. They exited the truck but this time Livi did not give Jake the chance to open her door, and she got out and rounded the front of the truck before he could take a step in her direction. Nevertheless, he was first to reach the front door and opened it for her, grinning as he beat her at her game. She smiled at him playfully as she crossed the guesthouse threshold.

The front door opened to a large kitchen complete with a hefty, rustic farmhouse table accompanied by two, long, wooden benches and a massive stone fireplace. Not much had changed in the kitchen since Livi had last visited the guesthouse, and the dated stove and refrigerator still shouted their avocado green color. Livi surveyed the room noting that the new stainless steel sink shone brightly in contrast with the darkly paneled cabin walls and beamed ceiling. The room still had a musty smell, and Livi imagined the old farmhands sitting around the table eating biscuits and gravy.

"Obviously, this is still the kitchen," Jake said as he closed the front door behind them. "I added that new sink and plan to replace these old green appliances with stainless steel models. I am still working on where to place the microwave." Jake pointed to the hallway off the kitchen and continued, "Back here Dad added another bathroom to the right and of course the bunkroom is beyond that. While I am here, I'm going to update the bathrooms with new tile, and I think I have room to add a shower in one. Eventually I hope to divide the bunkroom into a study and two smaller bedrooms. That seems more practical." Jake's arms were pointing in every direction with his excitement as he rattled off his renovation details.

"That sounds great. Is Nell going to help with the decorating?" Livi asked. She thought Jake talked as if he might stay in Millersville longer than "a while."

"I haven't gotten that far. I really don't know how long I'm going to be here so I'm just working on what I can for now. Dad has not decided if he wants to sell the guesthouse or just rent it out. Either way, these updates are necessary to make it marketable. I guess you can tell I am pretty excited to have a new construction project." Jake grinned and walked over to the avocado green refrigerator. "I don't have any wine here. Would you like a beer?"

"Sure." *More alcohol couldn't hurt,* she thought. Livi mentally noted that Jake remembered she was a wine drinker.

Jake grabbed two Coors Light bottles and motioned for Livi to follow him to the back porch. The porch spread the length of the guesthouse and its only inhabitants were two old ladder-backed rocking chairs facing the river. The brilliantly colored sunset peeked through the branches of an ancient oak tree which sat midway between the porch and the riverbank.

Jake pointed to the grassy area nearest to the back porch and said, "Here I am going to add an outdoor kitchen if Dad's budget allows. I got used to eating under the stars in Iraq, so now I want an outdoor kitchen wherever I go."

"Speaking of Iraq, I'm sorry about Ben," Livi said as she crossed the porch to stand beside Jake.

Livi's reference to their old friend suddenly caused Jake's excitement level to plummet and he turned away from her, leaving Livi facing the river alone. Ben had been gone almost a year now but the mention of his friend's name sucked Jake's enthusiasm right out of his voice.

"Thanks. I appreciated your sympathy card. It has been tough. I saw a lot of good guys get blown away over there. I just never imagined my best friend would be one of them."

"Well, he would love what you are doing with this place." Livi regretted mentioning Ben and tried to bring the conversation back to Jake's guesthouse plans.

"Yeah, we made a lot of good memories here." Jake turned and pulled the two rockers closer to the edge of the back porch. "Here, take a seat."

Livi sat and from her new vantage point she could see the gleaming sunset sliding below the oak's huge branches and begin to kiss the horizon. Jake stared at the river in silence and Livi assumed he was still thinking of Ben. They rocked for a while, each sipping their beer and watching the sun slowly set.

"This is nice." Livi tried to bring the conversation around again before Jake closed up completely. She remembered how easily he distanced himself when his mind focused on anything unpleasant. "I don't get to relax like this often."

"Yeah, I hear you're working a lot." Jake's brief sentence was evidence he had already started his closing up ritual.

"You heard right, but I enjoy it. The pace is fast and exciting, and there is no better feeling than closing a big deal." Livi was working hard to keep the conversation going.

"Really? No better feeling? I didn't know corporate work was that fulfilling," Jake said.

"Well, I. . .I like it. It keeps me busy." Livi did not mean to sound defensive.

"Too busy to do much else from what I hear. Nell says she never sees you out except at her store." Jake looked straight ahead as he took a long swig of beer.

Livi had no rebuttal to Jake's comment and she knew his bluntness meant he had officially closed up. They continued to rock in silence until the sun vanished completely and the beer bottles were bone dry.

Abruptly, Jake rose from his rocker, interrupting their silence. "Well, you have work tomorrow so I better get you back. I really just wanted to show you the guesthouse and now you have seen it, so let's head out."

He took Livi's empty beer bottle and headed inside. Livi followed him into the kitchen, wishing she had never mentioned Ben or work. Both had been buzz kills. He held open the front door and she walked down the front porch stairs to her side of the truck. This time Jake was not there to play the part of gentleman, so she opened her truck door herself and got in just as Jake started the engine. It was official. Jake had closed up and her butterflies had flown the coop.

The ride home was quiet and Livi was not sure whether Jake's silence resulted from thoughts of Ben or he simply had nothing to say to her. They were from two different worlds now so maybe they really did not have much in common. She was a focused career woman and he was ex-military without any ties to anywhere.

Their lack of conversation tonight was evidence of their lack of commonality and Livi's thoughts roamed in the silence of the truck. Maybe Jake's silence was a sign of his disapproval. He probably did not like what she had become. Livi was an expert at rationalizing, and in the silence of the ride home she had convinced herself that Jake was disappointed with her life's outcome and truly only thought of her as an old friend. *An old friend with no life*, Livi thought. His assumed disapproval hurt Livi and she was glad the ride would soon be over.

"Well, here we are." Jake pulled up in front of Livi's house and turned to face her. "Look, I'm sorry I closed up back there but Ben has a way of doing that to me when he gets in my head." High school Jake would never have admitted this. Perhaps present-day Jake's maturity had opened him up a little.

"No problem," Livi now knew the root of Jake's silence and she was relieved it was not her.

"Look, this night did not go the way I planned so . . .uh. . . could we try this again . . . maybe on a day when we have more time and work isn't hanging over your head? This time I promise to be more fun." Jake's green eyes sparkled in the streetlights and Livi felt herself getting lost in them again.

"Absolutely. I'd love to see you again." There. Livi said it. She would love to see him again. Perhaps present-day Livi had opened up a little herself as she felt her butterflies swooping in for another landing.

"Fantastic. Are you working this Saturday?" Jake sounded excited again.

"No. Saturday is perfect." She could give up one Saturday for Jake. Work would still be there.

"Then it's a date. I will pick you up at nine that morning, sharp. And for the record," Jake paused and grabbed her hand, "I'd love to see you again, too." Jake smiled as he got out of his truck and walked over to her door. This time, he opened it for her and held her arm as she jumped out.

They walked to her front door passing Gatsby waiting inside at the front bay window. They turned to face each other, each smiling a knowing smile. Jake squeezed Livi's hand, winked at her and bounded off to his truck before she could squeeze back or say a word. She waved and thought she could see him still smiling as he drove off.

He called it a date, Livi thought as she opened her front door. She ruffled the fur on Gatsby's head as they both headed back to her bedroom for the night. Once in bed, she could not sleep, but instead of counting sheep, she counted the hours until she could see Jake again.

Chapter Five

The next morning as she drove to work, Al Green sang "Let's Stay Together" louder than usual in Livi's car. The former Reverend Green had always been her dad's favorite and his music was ingrained in Livi's persona. The seventies soul man playing on her dad's stereo after he got home from work was an indication that Mr. Miller had been especially creative at his drafting table that particular day.

Thus, thanks to her father's creative success as an architect, Livi had learned every word to every song in her younger days. Al Green was Livi's happy place and she had not been there in a while. So it was quite a shock to Hampton Steel's front desk receptionist when Livi walked in that morning singing "Love and Happiness" out loud.

"Somebody had a good night. Anybody I know?" asked Barbara, Hampton Steel's long-time receptionist. She was the stereotypical large, southern, African-American woman and knew everything about everybody. Some even thought she secretly ran the place. She knew which executives required proper behavior and which ones allowed her to be herself. Livi was the latter and the two women had developed a special relationship over the years.

Livi smiled coyly. "No. Just in a good mood," she said, feigning ignorance.

"Well, I haven't seen that in a long while. Either you got yourself a man or that big promotion everybody's talking about is coming up."

"Now, Ms. Barbara, I just don't know what you are talking about," Livi said in her best Scarlett O'Hara drawl as she headed for her office leaving behind Barbara cackling in the lobby.

*

As usual, Nadine was already at her desk. "Here are your messages, and Robert wants to see you sometime late this afternoon." Nadine looked up from her computer. Livi's glow was unmistakable, and Nadine actually caught herself feeling a touch jealous at how good Livi looked this morning. "What'd you do? Did you do something different with your make-up?" the young assistant questioned.

"No," Livi grinned and continued walking into her office. But within seconds she came right back. "Okay. I have to tell someone. Guess who I was with last night?" she gushed.

"Who?" replied Nadine.

"Jake Cooper."

"Wow. Now there's a blast from the past," said Nadine. Her jealously level rose a bit. For Nadine, Jake had always been one of the good guys she wanted to date but never had a chance because she had been too busy "getting busy" with everyone else. Besides, Jake had always belonged to Livi. Everyone knew that. "How'd that happen?"

"I ran into him the other day at Nell's. He's in town visiting his parents and fixing up their guesthouse. He took me out there to see it last night." Livi smiled with memories of the night before.

"The guesthouse, huh? Lot of memories there," said Nadine. Actually, too many for her. Some of Jake's friends had liked "getting busy," too, and the guesthouse had been their preferred arena.

"Yeah. I was nervous about seeing him, but it was not as bad as it could have been. We're getting together Saturday, too."

"To do what?" Nadine unintentionally sounded snippy.

"I don't know, but he called it a date," said Livi. The preoccupied young attorney seemed not to have caught her assistant's snippiness.

"If he called it a date, you need a new outfit. Let's handle that during lunch today," said Nadine. Outwardly, she quickly recovered back into the role of loyal assistant, but inside her jealousy level was still up there.

"Great!" Livi headed back to her office.

Nadine dutifully sat at her desk staring at her computer but she could not concentrate on her work. *First the promotion, now Jake. Talk about having it all,* she thought.

Nadine was working for a woman who could not have a bad day to save her soul. And what was Nadine doing? Sitting at the same computer she had for years, going to the same local bars, drinking with the same guys. There had to be more out there for her. Nadine just did not know how to speed up her plan to get it.

By the time lunchtime rolled around, Nadine was feeling a little better. She had spent the morning mentally reviewing which of her attributes were better than or equal to Livi's, and overall Nadine had come out on top. She still possessed certain qualities that guaranteed her free drinks whenever she went out. These qualities did not come easily and she viewed keeping up appearances as a second job. This second job forced her to religiously work out as well as maintain a professionally stocked cosmetic counter at her apartment. After comparing her body to Livi's, Nadine's cattiness was going to enjoy shopping for clothes with her boss during lunch.

Uncharacteristically, Livi and Nadine left for lunch together at exactly noon.

"If anyone needs me, just call my cell," Livi told Barbara as she and Nadine giggled across the front lobby. Barbara did a double-take as they walked out the front door. The two ladies normally did not take lunch at all, and to leave both their offices empty in the middle of the day was usually unthinkable for Livi.

*

As they found a prime parking spot downtown, Livi and Nadine had no intentions of actually eating lunch today. Nadine never ate lunch, feeling that skipping that meal each day helped her maintain her obligatory size four and, while Livi usually ate Hampton Steel's cafeteria food at her desk, today the butterflies had returned and there was no room in her digestive tract for anything else. They hit Millersville's most popular woman's boutique first, with Nadine browsing the cocktail dress racks and Livi looking for something casual.

"So what are we looking for?" asked Nadine when she realized they were not on the same page for date clothes. *And of course our sizes are not the same at all,* thought Nadine.

Livi responded, "I don't know. I haven't done this in a while. Jake just said he's picking me up at nine in the morning on Saturday." Livi looked at the dress Nadine was holding up and remarked, "I assume we are not going out for cocktails on a Saturday morning. Besides, you know I can't wear a size four."

Nadine did not reveal her satisfaction as she turned to place the dress back on the rack. She had gotten her jab in and felt better even if Livi was oblivious to it all. "Nine in the morning? Sounds like he is planning a day of it. We might as well get something that can take you from day into night in case it goes *really* well," Nadine said as she winked.

Livi blushed. "Nadine!"

"I'm just saying you never know what will happen and a girl must always be prepared," Nadine said, speaking from experience.

*

They hit a few more clothing stores downtown, trying to avoid the typical retail chains, but ultimately Livi settled on brown corduroy pants and a blue cable sweater from Ann Taylor Loft. The blue matched her eyes and, of course, the sweater covered her butt in the back with the V-neck emphasizing her well-endowed breasts in the front.

Livi knew it was similar to what she had worn the other night but she really did not care. It was new and made her feel pretty and, according to Nadine, that was all that really mattered. New sunglasses and a purse completed her shopping excursion, and she returned to the office feeling more like a teenage girl than a Hampton Steel executive.

As they entered Hampton Steel's lobby, the Armani stranger from the general counsel's office the day before was passing Barbara's desk and heading toward the front door. As he walked toward Livi and Nadine, Livi glanced at his shoes. Just as she thought, Armani again.

Mr. Armani nodded and smiled at the ladies with his glance lingering over Nadine, of course, as he left the building. The glance did not go unnoticed by Nadine and she smiled back at Armani, tossing back her long blonde hair and standing up just a little bit straighter as she feigned a blush.

"Who was that?" Livi asked Barbara after Armani was out the door.

"Have no idea. He's been here visiting the big wigs. Just signs in as 'Winston' and goes on up. Executive Floor just told me to let him in whenever he is here. He just heads upstairs like he owns the place. He doesn't say much. Just flashes his smile like I'm supposed to know who he is. He is either snooty or Yankee, I can't tell which," said Barbara, obviously irritated she did not know more about Armani.

"Well, I'm sure we'll find out soon enough." Livi brushed aside her curiosity as she and Nadine headed back to their offices. She could not deal with Armani now. She had a date with Jake that needed her full attention.

That afternoon, Livi did not get much work done. She stayed in her office and luckily had very few interruptions. It was a beautiful fall afternoon and only the truly dedicated were still hanging around Hampton Steel. Without the customary, constant interruptions, Livi's mind wandered, replaying the other night with Jake for a while, then writing and rewriting the screenplay for their time together on Saturday. She had not looked forward to something with this much intensity for a long time, and her butterflies had become as familiar as Gatsby to the point that she thought she might start naming each one.

*

The man in the Armani suit sped out of the Hampton Steele

parking lot. He did not stop at the crosswalk and barely missed hitting six Hampton Steele employees returning from lunch. According to the dealer, Edward Winston drove the only Mercedes Benz SLS AMG Roadster in a ninety mile radius so he believed everyone should naturally get out of *his* way.

He was the one with the power now. He controlled Hampton Steele. And meeting with the general counsel for the umpteenth time today only confirmed to him that this town was rife with opportunity. If all the Hampton Steele executives were as gullible as the general counsel, Edward could complete his business in no time and be well on his way out of Millersville.

That had been his goal. To wrap things up and get out of town before anyone figured him out. But, after seeing the attractive blonde in the lobby this afternoon, he did not feel as rushed to reach his goal as he did before. Edward had a weak spot for blondes and this girl's endowed attributes were far superior to those of his wife. As he sped through Millersville's back roads, Edward decided he would take his time now. He would execute his plan for Hampton Steele slowly and methodically. And, in the midst of executing his plan, maybe he could fit in a little extracurricular activity with the blonde on the side.

*

Nadine went through the motions of the remaining workday while silently obsessing about her life. Livi's recent luck gnawed at Nadine. *There is definitely more to life than this,* she thought. Nadine always thought of herself as a big city woman stuck in small town America. After her second divorce, Nadine had written down a detailed plan for the rest of her life, and she believed Hampton Steel was her ticket out of Millersville. She just took this job as executive assistant to get her foot in the door.

Her plan was to eventually transfer out of legal and into sales.

As a Hampton Steel sales rep with a background in legal she thought she would obviously be the perfect candidate to take over one of Hampton Steel's larger sales regions, maybe Chicago or New York. Then, of course, she would move out of Millersville and her life would be set.

The first phase of her master plan was easy. Her "qualifications" and a few choice open button holes in her blouse had assured her a foot in the door since she had gotten busy with Hampton Steel's hiring manager before she took the job. The second phase, however, was taking a bit longer and she secretly blamed Livi for her inability to transfer out of legal.

Livi's constant compliments of Nadine in front of management had only pigeon-holed the ambitious assistant into Hampton Steel's legal department. No one, not even Livi, could see her sales potential. So, sitting at her computer that Friday afternoon, Nadine decided right then and there that she needed to change her plan. She did not know what kind of change or how. She just knew she needed to start doing something differently to kick start her life because what she was doing now was not working.

In the middle of this great realization, Nadine's phone rang and broke her concentration. It was the general counsel's assistant. The big man was ready to see Livi.

"Liv, Robert is ready for you now," Nadine called into Livi's office without leaving her desk.

"Be right there," Livi called to Nadine as she gathered her legal pad and pen. "This might be it. Keep your fingers crossed," she said as she rushed past Nadine's desk.

Nadine sarcastically smiled and thought, *Yeah, right. Your promotion is all I think about.* Nadine sighed and started going through the motions of her day again.

*

Livi took the elevator to the top floor of the building. Everyone called it the "Executive Floor" because it housed the Board Room as well as the offices of the CEO, CFO, COO and anyone else whose title was too long to actually spell out.

Stepping out of the elevator, Livi felt like she was stepping back in time to an office on Wall Street with its rich mahogany paneling, crystal chandeliers and large leather club chairs. Large Impressionist paintings, including an original Renoir, were framed in gold leaf and covered the walls of the executive foyer. Every time she visited this floor, Livi imagined J.P Morgan or one of the Vanderbilts sitting there smoking a cigar and barking orders.

Offices flanked both sides of the long hallway leading from the foyer to the Board Room, and the general counsel's suite was the second one on the right. To get to her boss, Livi had to first pass through the office of his assistant who acted as gatekeeper for all entering his domain. The assistant was protective of the general counsel and did her job well. Luckily, she liked Livi, so Livi had never encountered the mother bear side of her personality.

"Hello. Nadine said he wanted to see me," Livi said to the protective assistant.

"Hey, sweetie. I'll tell him you are here," said the assistant as she picked up the phone. "Mr. Matthews, Livi's here." Nothing could be heard through the thick mahogany door that separated the assistant from her boss but the general counsel obviously granted Livi permission to enter his inner sanctum because his assistant motioned her inside.

Livi opened the large door and found her boss, Robert Livingston Matthews, sitting behind his massive antique desk. Despite the stuffy atmosphere and corporate hierarchy, she felt comfortable in his office. While the décor mirrored that of the executive foyer, including a ceiling that rose twelve feet, Robert shared Livi's love of antiques and his taste had only enhanced the ambiance of the room.

She had spent many a late night working here with him so the grandeur of his office did not intimidate her. They had developed a relationship akin to that of uncle and niece, and she enjoyed working for him despite his penchant for alcohol. It was the basis of that relationship that prompted Robert to walk over and give her a hug that afternoon, disregarding all human resource guidelines which dictated a male boss should never touch a female employee out of fear of harassment allegations. Robert was too much of a gentleman to do anything harassing, and Livi liked the fact he was still old school enough to give hugs.

"So, how's my favorite lawyer? Congratulations on closing the Turnkitt deal. Fifty million dollars is nothing to sneeze at," Robert said proudly as he smiled and walked back to his desk. He was in his early sixties, pleasantly plump, balding and dressed in a three-piece suit every day. A product of Yale undergrad and Harvard law, he had been a star in his day. He helped build Hampton Steel up to the success of today, despite his numerous clashes with Hampton Steel's other board members.

Over the years, Hampton Steel's board had walked a fine line on certain legal issues and Robert did not always agree with the way the other board members voted. Livi believed these constant clashes, along with the knowledge that Hampton Steel did not always act within the boundaries of the law, had prompted her boss to drink in excess. Nevertheless, at one time in the distant past he had been a great legal scholar and truly enjoyed passing his wisdom on to younger attorneys, especially Livi. He had taught her a lot and, in return, she had covered for him on more than one occasion with the board of directors.

Livi smiled. "Thanks, boss. I'm just glad to see Turnkitt close before the end of the year." Livi sat across from him in her usual chair.

"It's a good feeling, isn't it? Closing a deal, thinking you are ensuring the company's future," Robert said, leaning back in his desk chair with his arms folded across his chest and resting on his protruding stomach.

"Yes, sir. Absolutely." *Where is he going with this?* thought Livi.

"I remember that feeling. Loved it! Nothing better." Robert abruptly sat up, turned around, and pulled a cigar out of the tabletop humidor on the credenza behind his desk. "Those were the days. Now here I am, being pushed into retirement and having no idea what thrills lay ahead," lamented Robert as he bit down hard on the thick cigar.

Livi's butterflies were back. *Is this it? Is my promotion coming today?* she anxiously thought.

"You know how much I like and respect you, Livi," Robert continued. "You are bright and have done and are going to do well in life."

"Yes, sir. Thank you, sir," said Livi, unconsciously and nervously popping her knuckles discretely in her lap.

"Now, you know the Board and I don't always agree. Sometimes they win, sometimes I win. With everything going on, you know that no matter what happens I will always take care of you. You do know that, don't you?" asked Robert.

"Yes, sir," said Livi. She had no clue what he was talking about. *With everything going on? Where is he going with this?* she thought.

"All your hard work in the past has not gone unnoticed. I know it hasn't been easy and I, of all people, understand your personal sacrifices. Shoot, I have three divorces to prove my personal sacrifices to this company. At least you haven't made that mistake!" Robert said with a laugh. "Anyway, I just wanted to thank you for your loyalty to me and to Hampton Steel and to assure you that your financial future is safe with me. Well, that's all for now." He stood up. Their meeting was obviously concluding. "Again, congrats on the closing and have a good night."

"Thank you, sir." Livi smiled, shook his hand and headed out the large, mahogany door. *What just happened? Am I promoted or not?* Livi thought, confused. She glanced at Robert's assistant as she headed to the elevator but the assistant did not look up from her computer. Robert had assured Livi that her financial future was safe. Was he referring to her promotion?

As she rode the elevator to her floor, Livi replayed the meeting over and over in her mind. Her expert rationalization skills soon kicked in and by the time she reached her office, she had convinced herself the promotion was in the bag. Why else would Robert be so complimentary of her? He was just waiting for the right time to officially announce it. He was obviously feeling nostalgic so maybe he was having a hard time facing retirement. He did mention he did not know what thrills lay ahead. Well, whatever the reason, she could wait on his announcement. Robert had been good to her. If he needed to take some extra time to announce his retirement and her obvious promotion, he could take it. She was not going anywhere.

Chapter Six

Livi woke Saturday morning with nothing but Jake on her mind and butterflies in her stomach. She had a leisurely evening with Gatsby the night before and her anticipation over her date with Jake had pushed out any thoughts of work, including her promotion and the strange meeting with Robert Matthews.

Jake would be picking her up in a little over an hour and she wanted plenty of time to prepare for the day, especially if Nadine was right and it could turn into a nighttime excursion as well. By the time Livi had plucked and primped and looked at herself and her new outfit in the mirror a thousand times, it was nine o'clock and Jake was knocking at her door. She was getting used to her butterflies now and was happy to feel them as she opened the door to see Jake smiling bigger than he had the other day.

"Hey, Liv. Are you ready?" asked Jake. He again wore jeans and a flannel shirt but Livi did not care. He would even look good in MC Hammer's parachute pants right about now.

"Sure." Livi grabbed her coat and new purse and turned to Gatsby, giving the mutt a head rub. "Be a good boy. I'll be back later," Livi said as she headed out the door.

"Why don't we take him with us? If you work as much as I hear you do, Gatsby needs an outing as much as you do," Jake said with a grin.

"Are you sure?" Livi knew she could not say "no" to Jake's smile but she still did not know what they were doing today. Would Gatsby be in the way? She did not want anything in her way today.

"Absolutely. He'll be fine. You know I am a sucker for a pouty face. Just look at him," said Jake pointing to the dog at his feet. Gatsby was sitting there staring at both of them as if he knew they were talking about him. He did look as if he was pouting a little, so Livi conceded and before she knew it they were all in the cab of Jake's truck with Gatsby drooling and happily sitting in the middle, staring out the truck's front window.

"It's supposed to be gorgeous today so I thought we could head to the river and do a little fishing. You do remember how to fly-fish don't you?" Jake knowingly asked.

"I haven't fished in forever but I always like a challenge. Sounds great," Livi lied. She had not had time for fishing in years. Even though she had fished every inch of the river with either Jake or her father when she was younger, time at work had taken away that part of her life. She hoped she could remember how to cast and did not want to look like an idiot in front of Jake.

As if reading her mind, Jake said, "Casting is like riding a bicycle. You never forget. Besides, from what I remember, you were a natural so you shouldn't have any problems."

Jake drove for a while and finally stopped at Dan Jenkins's local fly shop. Like the other night, Jake was quick to round the truck and open her door. Gatsby hopped out with them and entered the store alongside the young couple.

Jake and Livi were familiar with the old fly shop because it had been somewhat of a hangout for the teenagers when they were in high school. It catered to the novice as well as the old pro and had a reputation for being the best-stocked fly shop in the region. It stayed busy almost year round thanks to this reputation but also because it was the closest beer run for the local river's best fishing spots.

"Well, as I live and breathe," said the man behind the counter. "Livi Miller and Jake Cooper in my shop—together. Talk about a blast from the past. What are you two strangers doing here?"

Dan Jenkins was an old, close friend of Mr. Miller and had been on the river with him the day Livi's father found out about her mother's accident. He had stayed with Mr. Miller in his grief, taking care of him while Livi made the lonely four-hour drive home from Charlottesville and, for that reason, Livi considered

Dan one of the special people in her life. The burly man knew everything there ever was about fly-fishing and was quite the local celebrity around Millersville because of this knowledge. As the old fisherman came out from behind the counter, Livi was reminded what a large man he was. Dan gave Livi a huge hug and his outdoor smell reminded her of her father.

"Hey, Dan. Good to see you," Jake said as he shook the large man's hand. "I'm back in town for a while and was able to get Livi out of the office so we are taking advantage of today's weather and plan on doing a little fishing. Thought you could set us up with some flies."

"Well, I'm glad someone could get Livi out of that glass box she calls work," Dan said, turning to Livi. "I told your father the other day how much I missed seeing you. Glad to see Jake can get you outside." Dan was relentless and enjoyed giving Livi a hard time.

"Now, Dan. It hasn't been that long," Livi said, sounding defensive.

"Yes, it has! I was beginning to think you didn't love me anymore," Dan joked.

"I still love you. It's tolerating you I have a hard time with," said Livi, joking right back.

"All right. I'll stop teasing you today if you promise to come see me more. Now, let's hurry up and get you two outside. Where are you fishing today?" Dan asked Jake.

"I thought we'd just head up to the section of river that runs behind our farm, about a mile up from the guesthouse. Do you know what's been biting up there?" Jake asked Dan, without taking his eyes off Livi.

Oh please, don't let me blush right now, thought Livi as she clutched her stomach in an unsuccessful attempt to control her butterflies.

"Hmm," said Dan as he headed to the fly case. "Haven't been up there in a while but the last time I was there, the fish were biting pretty good on these." Dan pointed to a row of flies in the case.

"Well, set us up then." Jake turned to Livi. "Is that okay with you, Livi?"

"Sure." Livi really had no idea what was okay as far as flies go and she honestly didn't care so long as she could spend the day in Jake's smile.

"Well, here you go," said Dan as he handed the bag of flies to Jake. "Do you need anything else?"

"No, we're covered. I've got everything else in my truck. What do I owe you?" Jake asked.

"Nothing. They're on the house. I'm just glad to see Livi back on the river again." Dan smiled at Livi and gave Gatsby his head rub. "You all come back and bring pictures of what you catch today," the old fisherman requested.

"Sure thing, Dan. Thanks," said Jake as he shook Dan's hand again and opened the shop door for Livi and Gatsby.

"Thank you, Dan," said Livi as she gave him another hug. She turned and flashed the old man a smile as the three headed out the door and into the truck.

"I didn't know your workaholic reputation was so widespread," joked Jake once they were on the road again.

"Oh, Dan just thinks everyone should spend every second on the river fly-fishing. He doesn't understand that some of us actually have to work for a living. He just enjoys giving me a hard time," Livi brushed off her well-founded reputation.

"He obviously missed seeing you. I think a lot of people miss seeing you," Jake said with intent in his eyes. He smiled at Livi again and she felt her heart melt as the butterflies swooped around inside her. They drove for a while in silence listening to the local station on the truck's old radio.

They were both obviously lost in their own memories of each other and the music helped fuel the reminiscing fires. By the time they turned onto Jake's road, both felt like high school sweethearts again and were reveling in that young feeling.

Jake drove past the Coopers' farmhouse and then the guesthouse and finally stopped the truck on the river bank about a mile down the gravel road. "Is this okay?" Jake asked.

"Sure," Livi said.

Jake opened Livi's door, looked at Gatsby and said, "He won't run away, will he?"

"No. He'll be fine. He doesn't stray far from the hand that feeds him." Livi appreciated Jake's concern for her dog.

"Speaking of food, I had to guess what you would be hungry for," said Jake as he lifted a picnic basket and blanket from the back of the truck. "Do you still like turkey and cheese or have your tastes gotten more sophisticated now that you are a big-time Hampton Steel executive?" Jake asked, grinning.

"I'm good with anything you brought," Livi replied knowing her butterflies left no room in her stomach for food. She and her new friends were loving Jake's attention.

They headed to a nearby oak tree and spread the blanket under its long limbs. The oak leaves were already displaying their fall brilliance, and their bright orange color made the large, round tree look as if the sun had drifted down from the sky to rest right there on the riverbank. Not appreciating the romantic setting that the tree established on the riverbank, Gatsby immediately sprawled out in the middle of the blanket, leaving no room for either Jake or Livi to sit down.

"Sorry about that. Gatsby thinks we were all put on this earth to serve him." Livi laughed.

"No problem. I'm not hungry yet, anyway. Are you?" asked Jake.

"No, I'm fine." Livi's butterflies fluttered in her stomach.

"So, Gatsby can nap and we'll brush up on our fly-fishing skills." Jake headed to the truck and pulled out his gear from the back. "You know Ben and I actually tried to fish a little in Iraq. It wasn't the same. Our Virginia mountains are so much better," Jake looked over at Livi, "Do you want me to help with your flies?"

"Absolutely. Tying flies was never one of my better skill sets," admitted Livi. She was glad Jake had gotten past his Ben issues of the other night.

They headed to the river bank and Jake set up Livi's rod, reel and flies as she took off her shoes to put on the booted waders Jake had packed for her. He had thought of everything and handed her the rod ready for her to cast. She did not want to look stupid, so she waded into the river as if she remembered what she was supposed to do. She stood far enough away from the tree so her line would not get caught in its branches. At least she remembered that much from her younger fishing days. Jake quickly put on his waders and quietly waded into the river on the other side of the tree's branches, keeping his distance so that his line would not get caught in Livi's. Unfortunately, this distance also prevented any conversation between them across the river's waters. *Oh, well. So much for talking about old times today*, thought Livi disappointedly.

Livi watched Jake cast a few times before his line settled on top of the river. She could only imagine his muscles flexing and moving beneath his flannel shirt, and thoughts of Jake's toned body made some of the butterflies leave Livi's stomach and settle down between her upper thighs.

She had not felt anything in that area of her body in a long while and was surprised at how easily excited she was by Jake's movements. Livi hoped Jake could not see her blush from his vantage point and decided she needed to focus on the fishing before she had an orgasm right there on the river. As she started concentrating on her casting, the butterflies moved back to her stomach and she knew she had dodged a close one.

Her mind was now set to make the perfect cast but Jake had been wrong. Casting was not like riding a bicycle and her line was going everywhere but where she wanted it to. After what felt like an eternity, Jake looked over to see her struggling. He immediately waded to the riverbank, laid down his rod and moved back out into the river toward Livi.

"You look good," Jake lied to make her feel better. "You just need to remember the ten and two. When you cast, pretend your arm is like an arm of a clock. Just don't move it past ten o'clock or two o'clock." Jake took Livi's rod and demonstrated.

As she watched Jake's movements, her butterflies were again packing for their trip down south to Livi's upper thighs so she squeezed her legs together hoping that might close the door on her butterflies' migration.

"Now you try," said Jake handing the rod to Livi. She cast a few times and the line landed a little better but not by much.

"Here, this may help," said Jake as he stepped behind her, putting his arms around her, holding the rod with his hands on top of her hands. He guided her arms and body back and forth, practicing laying her line on the water while his cheek brushed her cheek with each cast. They swayed together in unison and she could feel his heart pounding as his chest enveloped her back. Looking at him out of the corner of her eye, she caught him watching her face instead of the line.

Their faces were so close, one slight turn of their heads as they swayed and their lips could land in a kiss. Just when Livi thought they were headed in that direction, the line went taut and a large trout jumped out of the water. This inopportune stroke of fishing luck shocked them both and Livi let out a little scream. Her scream then woke up Gatsby who headed into the water toward her and the jumping trout. Livi immediately let go of the rod and rushed to coax Gatsby out of the water while Jake quickly and expertly reeled in her catch. *Just my luck*, thought Livi, *interrupted by a fish and a dog*.

"She's a beaut!" said Jake holding up the fish that so rudely intruded on them.

"Wow. Is that dinner?" Livi hinted, obviously not wanting this day to end.

"Normally I subscribe to the catch and release philosophy of fly-fishing, but today I can make an exception," Jake said as he waded up the riverbank toward Livi and Gatsby. He placed the fish in a cooler filled with water and began resetting their rods. Apparently they were going to fish more and Jake was ignoring Livi's dinner comment. They spent the remainder of the day on the river, with only a break every now and then to snack out of Jake's picnic basket, which luckily included wine.

Livi had forgotten how relaxing fly-fishing could be and she easily lost herself on the river while Gatsby dozed on the nearby blanket. She and Jake both caught their share of fish throughout the afternoon even though each spent more time stealing glances at each other than watching their lines. Jake's flashing smile kept her heart in continuous meltdown mode, and Livi decided that it was indeed a good day and one that she had not experienced in a very, very long while.

By late afternoon, both had their fill of fishing and started packing up the truck for the ride home. The fall sun was beginning to set and the evening wind was cooling down the riverbank. Jake caught Livi shivering a little as she stepped out of her waders, which were obviously not totally waterproof. Her new pants appeared to be a little more than damp but slightly less than drenched.

"Why didn't you tell me your waders were leaking?" Jake asked, surprised.

"It's no big deal. They'll dry eventually," she said. Livi was not about to let wet pants barge in on her day.

"You need a fire to dry those. How about we go back to the guesthouse and cook an early fish dinner? Did you have any plans for dinner?" asked Jake.

"No. No dinner plans. That sounds great," she responded. She tried to hide her excitement. Of course Livi did not have any other plans. Jake was her dinner plan.

The short drive to the guesthouse seemed to last forever to Livi. When they eventually pulled up, Gatsby jumped out of the truck and ran straight to the front door as if he knew exactly where he was going. Livi and Jake unloaded the truck after which Jake worked on the fire in the kitchen's fireplace while Gatsby staked his claim on a nearby blanket and took full advantage of the fire's warmth. Livi watched Jake heave the heavy wood around the hearth and felt her butterflies heat up again. She did not know where this was headed but she really liked the ride so far.

Jake turned around and caught her staring at him. "Okay. This is going to sound weird and I really don't mean anything by it, but let's get you out of those wet clothes," he said.

"Jake!" Livi tried to act embarrassed but deep down her butterflies were smiling.

"No. Calm down. I don't mean anything by that. Just wait a second," said Jake as he ran back to the bunkroom. He came back in a few seconds with a towel, sweatshirt and sweatpants. "Here. I'll cook dinner and you go take a bath to warm up. You can wear these while your pants dry by the fire."

Livi smiled. Jake had once again assumed the role of caretaker and she was glad. He had played that role well when they were together in high school, and she realized how much she had missed having someone else in charge of her wellbeing. It felt good to have Jake in control and Livi headed back to the bathroom and closed the door. The bath relaxed her even more and Livi stayed in the warm water longer than she intended. She washed away the river and fish smell that had settled in her hair and skin and finally arose from the tub like Botticelli's Venus, clean and feeling refreshed. The sweatpants and sweatshirt were naturally too big, but a roll of the cuffs and her ensemble was complete. Livi did what she could with her wet hair, but without her hairdryer, styling was a lost cause. Luckily, her purse contained enough make-up to make her once again feel pretty, so the style of her hair had no effect on her butterflies.

When she finally emerged from the bathroom, any doubt she had about Jake's feelings for her disappeared completely. There in the kitchen stood Jake at the avocado green stove with spatula in hand cooking trout while Gatsby sat on his chosen blanket. A fire roared in the fireplace and the room was aglow with candles spread all over the room. French vanilla scent filled the air and masked the trout's smell. The table was set for a candlelight dinner and Al Green was playing softly on the stereo. Livi's butterflies were overjoyed.

"Hey. You look like you feel better. Hope you don't mind the ambiance but lamps are scarce here in the guesthouse and I know how much you like Al Green. Thought we could listen to the Reverend while we eat." Jake's happiness was grinning from ear to ear.

"Jake, this is wonderful. Thank you," said Livi as she sat down at the large farmhouse table.

"Here you go," said Jake as he set the plates on the table. The plates were filled with the trout, some salad and bread. Wine had already been poured and he sat down across from Livi. He looked gorgeous in the candlelight which intensified the green of his eyes. "I didn't have much here for dinner but at least we are eating healthy," he continued.

"This looks great. More than I ever expected," she gushed. Livi's butterflies once again left no room for food.

"I think I may have a package of M&Ms somewhere around here for dessert. I remember how you like your chocolate," Jake said. He seemed to remember everything about Livi.

They ate in the candlelight and finished off the wine as they discussed their high school classmates and where everyone had ended up. Both tried to avoid any discussion that remotely touched on each other or their current romantic surroundings. Neither wanted to be pushy but deep down both were ecstatic with where they each found themselves at that moment. Before they knew it, their plates were clean and the wine bottle empty.

"So, are you ready for those M&Ms?" asked Jake as he carried both plates to the kitchen sink.

"No. I'll pass tonight. But I will clean up. You cooked so it's only fair that I deal with the mess," Livi said as she moved to the sink and grabbed the kitchen sponge.

"Liv. You don't have to do that. It's no big deal, really." Jake was standing so close to Livi he could smell her hair. They both reached down into the sink at the same time, causing their hands to lightly brush against each other.

That slight touch was too much for either of them in this romantic setting and Jake suddenly turned, grabbed Livi's arms and pulled her to him. His green eyes melted into her blue eyes as his words erupted. "Look, Liv. I've recently learned life is too short so here goes." He took a deep breath. "I love you. I've always loved you and never stopped loving you. I hated the way things ended between us. With your work schedule, I really did not expect to see you while I'm in town, but I did and here we are and I can't stop thinking about you. This was the best day I've had in a long time and it is all because I was with you. I'm sorry if this scares you but there it is. I said it. It's out in the open. Jake still loves Livi."

Livi stood there and was grateful Jake was holding her arms, otherwise she would have collapsed onto the kitchen floor right then and there. For once in her life she was speechless and she just stared into his green eyes, her butterflies racing laps from her stomach, to her head, to her thighs and back again.

She must have stood there too long because Jake said, "I. . .I'm sorry. I didn't mean to catch you so off guard. It. . . it just came out." He released her arms and turned back toward the sink.

"No! Don't be sorry!" Livi said as she flung her arms around his neck and pulled him back to her. Their bodies pressed against each other, with arms roaming every inch of their embrace. When their lips finally met, they each experienced the longest, hardest kiss either had felt since they were last together.

Jake's lips then softly moved up Livi's cheek, finding her ear and whispering, "Oh, Liv. Thank you. Thank you." They stood there kissing a long time when, finally, with one fluid motion, Jake picked Livi up and carried her back to the bunkroom where the only light was the fall moon glowing through the window. He laid her gently on his bed, Livi's dark hair flowing over his stark white pillow.

He held her tightly as he kissed her lips, then her cheeks, then her neck. Livi's thighs felt his hardness through his jeans and she let out a little groan as Jake's hands eventually moved under her sweatshirt and up her back, caressing every inch of her skin. Livi then slid her hands under the back of Jake's shirt and lightly massaged his skin with her fingers as she kissed his forehead. His tongue darted over and up her neck and their lips finally found each other again while their hands continued to roam. Jake's fingers finally made their way to Livi's bare stomach and slowly inched up to her breasts, feeling her nipples' hardness as her excitement rose.

He pulled up her sweatshirt even higher as his lips moved down her body, enveloping her breasts in a softness she had never known. He sucked and kissed and massaged her breasts while Livi's fingers ran through his hair as she pressed his face to her chest.

Without notice, Livi felt her excitement ready to explode and she arched her back, pushing her breast deeper into Jake's mouth. He held her tight, knowing what was coming and realizing that he too was ready to release his excitement. Their lips met again just as each exploded in ecstasy, both groaning in happiness while they clutched each other tightly.

Livi had never experienced anything like that before, having an orgasm while fully clothed. Her heart and mind were racing and she realized this was truly not expected when she started the day out. She leaned back out of Jake's arms, not sure what to do next.

"Don't move," Jake whispered as he pulled her back to him. "Please stay."

Livi rolled back into his arms as he pulled the bed's antique quilt up over both of them. The night sky cast a heavenly glow around them, and Livi thought she could see her butterflies free and dancing in the room's moonlight as she closed her eyes and fell asleep.

Chapter Seven

Livi awoke the next day to the smell of bacon and, at first, was slightly confused. Quickly remembering where she was amidst the familiarity of the rustic bunkroom, she smiled, closed her eyes and cuddled down into the warm quilt even further. *Man, am I happy*, she thought.

*

Jake heard Livi rustling back in the bunkroom and left the kitchen with Gatsby close on his heels. He stood in the bunkroom doorway staring at Livi nestled in his grandmother's antique quilt. *Man, am I lucky*, he thought.

He quietly returned to the kitchen and arranged Livi's breakfast on the only tray he could scrounge up from the sparsely equipped cabinets. It had pictures of Batman covering it and was a remnant of his elementary school days. The fall season did not provide any flowers to adorn Livi's tray so Jake included the bag of M&Ms as both a gesture and decoration. He carried the tray back to Livi whom he found lying in bed staring at the bunkroom ceiling.

*

"Your breakfast, m'lady," Jake said in his best fake British accent and then bowed.

"Too funny," Livi said as Jake placed the tray in her lap. "Does Queen Elizabeth like Batman also?"

"Thought you could stand a little nourishment after last night," he said as he leaned over and kissed her forehead, "which was wonderful by the way." Jake sat down at the end of the bed facing

Livi while Gatsby grabbed a spot on the floor.

Livi blushed. "Jake, I . . . I really did not mean for anything like that to happen. I had no idea you still felt that way." She paused and batted her blue eyes. "But, for the record, it was one of the most romantic nights of my life."

"Good. Maybe we can have another." Jake's happiness shone through his grin as he leaned over and gave Livi another kiss, this time on the cheek. "What were you thinking about when I came in?" he asked. "You seemed lost in the ceiling."

"I was just thinking how relaxed I was yesterday." Livi paused and took a deep breath. "And how very much I love you." There. She said it and she meant it. "If you only knew how twisted my stomach has been since I first saw you at Nell's. I didn't know until I saw you that day how much you still affect me," Livi continued as she sat up straighter. "Look, you made your speech last night. Now it's my turn. I don't know how long you are here and I don't care. But if yesterday is any indication, we owe it to ourselves to spend as much time together as possible while you are here. I don't care where this goes as long as I am with you today, in the present." Livi paused. "So there."

Jake laughed and said, "You've gotten quite assertive in your old age, haven't you? How can I say 'No' to that? So what is on your agenda for today? More work or could you squeeze in some time for me?" he asked with a grin.

"It's Sunday. You know I have to go to church or my dad will kick my butt. After church I was going to work, but I can skip it today. Why don't you go to church with me? Nothing has changed. We still sing the same hymns and the blue-hairs are still falling asleep during Pastor Tom's sermon. You'll feel right at home," she said hesitantly.

"I don't think so," Jake responded. "I haven't been to church since Ben died. Kind of feel like I fell out of favor with the Man Upstairs. I was a little more than mad at Him when He took Ben away."

"But God didn't take Ben away," Livi disagreed. "The men who bombed Ben's tank took Ben away." Livi could not believe what she was hearing. She and Jake had grown up in Millersville's First Baptist Church together. Jake had always been the one who had to make *her* go to church when they were dating. She could not imagine Jake losing his faith like this. "Maybe today's the day you come back to church—with me," Livi said as she tried to be convincing.

"Let me think about it over breakfast. Okay?" Jake said.

"Sure." Livi was disappointed.

"Do you really want me to go?" he asked.

"Yes," Livi said and again batted her long eyelashes knowing her blue eyes always got their way with Jake.

Jake sighed. "Okay, but, in return, after church you and Gatsby are now required to spend the whole day with me. Understood?" he playfully asked.

"Yes, sir," said Livi as she gave Jake her best military salute. Her work could wait just one more day.

"Now that is more like it, Private," said Jake as he went back to the kitchen to get his breakfast. They lounged around eating breakfast in bed, each content with the other. Jake even gave Gatsby his own bowlful of bacon and eggs on the floor next to the bed.

"Do you miss the military?" Livi asked. She was enjoying getting to know Jake again.

"I miss the guys," replied Jake. "I don't miss the guns. But I'm glad I did it. I think it made me mature a lot faster than I would have otherwise. How about you? Is the law all you thought it would be?"

Livi sighed. "Yes and no. I still love it, don't get me wrong. But the hours can be a drag. I didn't expect my career to be so all encompassing and for it to take so long to get my life started. I thought by now I'd be driving a few kids around in my mini-van."

"I see you more in an SUV," said Jake, not seeming to mind the kids comment at all.

"Well, whatever. SUV, mini-van, they're all the same. Work can be fulfilling though. I think I may be promoted to general counsel soon. My boss is retiring and I'm next up to take his place," said Livi as she sat up straighter in bed.

"That's great, Liv. I'm happy for you. Actually, I'm really proud of you. I always knew you'd do well," Jake said as he finished off the last of the bacon.

Livi knew Jake meant that and she decided that was enough talk about her work. "We better get going if we are going to make church on time. We still need to drop Gatsby off at my house," she said.

Jake showered and dressed while Livi cleaned up the kitchen from this morning's breakfast and last night's dinner. Jake did not like to wear suits, so he opted for khakis and a pullover sweater for church. Suit or not, Livi thought he looked gorgeous and she had to once again try to control her butterflies. They drove to Livi's house to drop off Gatsby, and she had just enough time to shower and change into her church clothes. With Jake in her living room waiting, Livi decided she felt a little more "girlie" today and chose a dress for church rather than her standard business suit. She walked into the living room and Jake stood up and kissed her cheek. "You look fantastic," he said, looking her up and down.

Livi blushed. No one had complimented her looks in such a long time she was not sure how to react. Smiling, she made her way to Jake's truck and, as he once again opened her door, she truly felt like Cinderella going to the ball.

First Baptist Church of Millersville was not only the largest church in town but also was housed in one of the most prominent historic buildings downtown. It sat on a hill overlooking the downtown area and was architecturally impressive with its large stone steps and tall Corinthian columns leading to the front entrance.

Three tall, heavy, wooden doors opened to the church's vestibule and enthusiastic greeters shook Livi's and Jake's hands as they entered that morning. Sunlight filtered through the ancient stained glass windows and cast a rainbow glow over the congregation already seated in the sanctuary. Jake and Livi made their way down the aisle to the Millers' usual pew, causing the jaws of Elizabeth, Todd and Mr. Miller to drop in unison as they scooted over to make room for the couple.

Elizabeth questioningly raised her eyebrows at Livi who mouthed "later" just as Pastor Tom appeared from behind the choir loft to take his place at the podium. Even Hampton Steel's receptionist, Barbara, appeared uncharacteristically shocked when she looked down from the choir loft to see Livi sitting so closely to the opposite sex.

Jake was solemn as the service progressed, and Livi could tell he was uncomfortable. She held his hand during the first prayer and when it was over he did not let go. She looked over at him and smiled, and their hands stayed clutched throughout the rest of the hour, making Livi's heart quiver just like in high school. Livi could not concentrate on Pastor Tom's sermon and her mind wandered around the church.

Her ancestors founded the First Baptist Church of Millersville, and she wondered how many other Miller women over the years had held hands with their beaus while ignoring the religious message of the day. She assumed the number to be too many to count since most of the Miller women had married in this church, thereby converting many a Presbyterian or Methodist boy into Baptist, whether the boy liked it or not.

*

After the service, the Miller family said their good-byes to Pastor Tom as they headed out the middle front door. Jake shook Pastor Tom's hand and turned to follow Livi out.

"Welcome home, son, and thanks for coming today," Pastor Tom said but he did not immediately let go of Jake's hand after giving him the two-handed shake. "I hope you come back real soon," the clergy concluded and smiled.

"Thanks, Pastor. Good to see you again," replied Jake sheepishly as if Pastor Tom knew he had strayed from the fold. Jake caught up with Livi and grabbed her hand again. Her touch comforted him right now. Being in church was not as bad as he had imagined, and, while he was still a little uncomfortable being there, he was almost relieved he had taken the step to attend for the first time in almost a year.

"Jake, good to see you," said Mr. Miller as the clan gathered at the bottom of the church steps.

"Good to see you too, sir," said Jake as he shook Mr. Miller's hand.

"Hey, Jake. I've missed you so much!" Elizabeth said. She gave him a hug. "You remember Todd, don't you?" Elizabeth did not give Jake time to answer before she continued, "Okay, where are we all going for lunch?" Elizabeth wanted to make sure Livi and Jake were joining them and did not want to give them an opportunity to escape.

"How about The Diner?" said Mr. Miller. "I'm buying."

*

Lunch was uneventful and everyone acted as if Livi and Jake had never been apart. Livi knew from the moment that her father offered to buy lunch that he approved wholeheartedly of her being with Jake again.

With the exception of Todd, each fell back into their old routines with Jake and Elizabeth playfully giving each other a hard time and Mr. Miller and Livi playing referee. Todd soon joined Jake in Elizabeth's ribbing while Mr. Miller watched and seemed happy that Livi and Jake had found each other again.

After lunch everyone went their separate ways with Livi and Jake heading to her house. The remainder of their day was filled with a long walk for Gatsby followed by a trip to the movies to see the latest James Bond installment. Both were fans of Ian Fleming, and a debate over the greatest Bond followed with Livi and Jake eventually agreeing Sean Connery was by far the best. The couple finally ended up at Livi's house for dinner, but unfortunately her pantry and refrigerator reflected her workaholic lifestyle.

"Don't you ever eat?" asked Jake as he looked in the pantry for sustenance for the third time as if somehow food had magically appeared in the two minutes since he last opened the pantry door. Cereal, fiber bars and a box of macaroni and cheese were not going to cut it and Jake was getting a little hungry. "How about ordering a pizza?" he asked.

"Perfect. I'll call it in and you build a fire. Are you still a pepperoni freak?" asked Livi, feeling a little embarrassed by her lack of domesticity. *Note to self, go to grocery this week!* she thought.

"Sure. But I'll eat anything so just order what you want. My taste buds are a little warped now after Iraq," joked Jake.

The pizza came and went as did a bottle of wine and the couple settled in front of the fire with Gatsby at their side. They sat in silence a long time, both content in the presence of the other.

"I'm glad I went to church with you today," Jake finally said.

"Me too. I think you showing up pleasantly shocked my family," said Livi as she laughed.

"Yeah," Jake continued, sounding serious. "You know, church wasn't as bad as I thought it would be. It's just that I've tried to avoid the whole religious thing and praying since Ben died. God didn't hear my prayers back then, so I fell into a slump thinking I wasn't on his radar to deal with."

"God heard your prayers when Ben died. He just has other plans for you, and Ben's death became part of those plans," Livi said, trying to be helpful.

"I guess I kind of knew that." Jake paused. "I never told you this but I was really grateful for the sympathy card you sent me when Ben died. I carried that thing all over Iraq. Every time I got depressed, whether it was about Ben or just being in the middle of that blasted desert and wishing I was home, I would pull out that card and think of you. You helped me through it, Liv. You really did."

"I had no idea. Why didn't you write or call or something?" she asked.

"I thought about it but I just figured you were with someone," Jake replied honestly. "Some doctor or lawyer or some other rich guy who had stolen your heart. I assumed the last thing you needed was to hear your high school boyfriend was still pining away for you all the way from Iraq. Who needs that when you are a big time attorney at Hampton Steel?" Jake chuckled and playfully nudged Livi.

"Yeah, right," Livi said as she smiled and rolled her eyes. Her butterflies were falling hard for Jake and Livi was right behind them. "Seriously, though. I would have liked to hear from you. Maybe I missed you, too," said Livi.

"Good to know," said Jake staring at the fire.

"So, can you stay?" Livi whispered, nestling into his arms.

"Of course," Jake said as he held her tighter.

Chapter Eight

The next morning Livi called Nadine at the office. "Hey, how was your weekend?" Livi asked, sounding more cheerful than usual.

"Fine—and yours?" Nadine asked. She was not a morning person.

"Great, thanks. Uh, can you let Robert know I'm going to take today off? I'll have my cell phone if anyone needs me," Livi said. She was trying to sound professional but it was difficult with Jake lying next to her.

"Uh, sure, no problem. Is there anything wrong?" Nadine said, obviously stunned. Livi never took time off.

"No. Everything's great. Just taking a day. That's all. Call me if you need me," said Livi as she hurriedly hung up the phone, preventing her assistant from prying any further. She turned to Jake who was looking quite content in her bed. They had slept all night just holding each other, each satisfied without giving in to their sexual urges.

Sex had never been part of their relationship before, despite their adolescent desires in high school, and the years they dated had made them experts in controlling their sexual urges. But adult sexual urges were far different from adolescent urges. Adult sexual urges had greater ramifications and lasting effects on the hearts involved. Effects that could be damaging. So, after a long talk the night before, both had agreed that consummating their relationship would only confuse matters and they had decided not to "go all the way" until they knew which way they were actually going.

Livi was still gearing up for her promotion, and Jake was secretly not sure where he fit into Livi's lifestyle. Nevertheless, both had agreed to take full advantage of the time they had now, and, thus, Livi's day off was a necessity as far as she was concerned.

After a leisurely breakfast, Livi escaped to her room to get dressed. Jake was still wearing his rumpled khakis from the previous day, and Livi hoped they did not run into anyone from church before he could change clothes at his house. Livi emerged looking more beautiful than ever with her long dark hair flowing over her back and her blue eyes sparkling.

"You'd look good in a gunny sack," Jake said.

"You're crazy," Livi blushed. "Okay, so, we fished on Saturday. Why don't we do something I'm good at today? How about shopping? We could snazzy up the guesthouse a little. What do you think?" she asked.

"Sounds good. But remember, I'm still a guy's guy—so no 'man-purses' for me. I do have an image to uphold. Got it?" Jake joked.

"Absolutely." Livi laughed.

They headed downtown, leaving Gatsby pouting at Livi's front window. After stopping at the linen store for what Jake called "unnecessary fancy towels", they finally ended up at Nell's.

"Hey, sis," said Jake as he held open the shop's door for Livi. Nell turned away from the display case she was working on and seemed pleasantly surprised to see the two enter as if they were a couple.

"Hey, bro. Didn't you wear that to church yesterday?" Nell asked, giving them both a hard time. She was never subtle.

"Okay, now, hush Nell," Livi said. "You don't need to point out the obvious. We're just here because Jake wants to get a few things for the guesthouse." Livi looked around and did not see her Imari platter. "Hey, where did my platter go? Don't tell me you already sold it!" Livi said, disappointed.

"Yep. It came and went. Sorry, sweetie," Nell said, but she did not really seem sorry.

Livi and Nell spent a long time reviewing the many options Nell's store had for the guesthouse. At first, Jake gave a few opinions, but since most were vetoed by the ladies he eventually gave up and settled into an overstuffed club chair to alternately watch them work and read the newspaper. In the end, his sister and Livi truly knew Jake's taste, and he was pleased with the items they finally chose. They loaded everything in the back of Jake's truck, including the club chair, and the couple drove out to the guesthouse.

Jake quickly showered and changed clothes while Livi started unloading the truck. She needed Jake to unload the heavier items, so she arranged what she could in the guesthouse until Jake emerged with a clean body and fresh clothes. As he lifted the club chair out of the truck, she could see his chest muscles flex beneath his tight, long-sleeved, tee shirt and her butterflies began making another trip down to her upper thighs. This "no-sex" thing was going to be harder than she thought.

Jake easily carried the club chair back to the bunkroom where his unmade bed screamed memories from the other night. After Livi positioned a newly purchased and much-needed lamp on the bedside table, she quickly began making up the bed, hoping to erase the scene she knew was simultaneously replaying in both their minds. As she bent over the bed to smooth out the antique quilt, she caught Jake staring at her as he sat in his new chair.

"What?" Livi asked.

"Nothing. I just like watching you," Jake said as he stood up and made his way to her. "I truly do love you. In fact, I never stopped loving you. You know that, right?" Jake said as he put his arms around Livi and pulled her close.

"And I love you," Livi said as her butterflies unpacked in her pelvis. "You know, you make this 'no-sex' thing very hard."

"You certainly don't make it easy either, missy," Jake joked as his hands moved inside her sweater to feel the soft skin of her back. He leaned down and kissed her, softly and slowly, savoring every ounce of wetness her mouth offered. She enjoyed his sweet kisses, and the feel of his tongue in her mouth. They stood there just kissing for a very long time and with each kiss their excitement levels rose until finally Jake stepped back and started removing his tee shirt.

"Wait. What are you doing? I thought we had an agreement," Livi said, surprised Jake was moving so fast after last night's discussion.

"It's okay," Jake whispered, holding her face in his hands. "I promise we won't break our agreement. I just need to feel your skin against mine." Jake's naked muscled chest caught Livi off guard and she did not know what to say or do. As Jake leaned in and once again took over her lips, Livi's mind went blank. She could feel Jake's fingers expertly unfastening her bra, which quickly slid to the floor along with her sweater.

Standing there half-naked with the midday sun streaming through the bunkhouse windows, Livi's self-consciousness threatened to ruin the moment. But as they stood there kissing in the sunlight, bodies pressed tightly together, skin touching skin, Livi was soon lost again in Jake's embrace as he lay her back on the quilted bed, his strong arms easing her down until her head landed in the feather-filled pillow.

Livi's breaths quickened with Jake's every move as he gently took off her boots and socks, tossing them to the floor. He then stood up and stripped off his own jeans and boots, leaving only his boxers to cover his hardness.

Seeing Jake standing there like that made Livi's butterflies flit around impatiently, tickling inside her upper thighs. Jake felt her excitement escalate with each breath, and he tenderly leaned over her on the bed, their eyes silently locked together as he unbuttoned her jeans and slowly pulled them down and off her legs. She lay there naked with just her panties on and instinctively tried to cover herself up with her hands and arms.

"Don't," whispered Jake as he sat back to look at her.

"I'm a little embarrassed. You know how I feel about being naked," Livi murmured in between breaths. She did not want Jake to see her body like this in the sunlight.

"I think you're beautiful," said Jake as he leaned down and kissed her full lips. They lay against each other kissing, skin on skin, with only underwear preventing them from breaking their agreement. Jake once again expertly moved down and maneuvered Livi's nipples with his tongue while his hands massaged her full breasts.

Livi's hands roamed his shirtless back and her legs wrapped around him tightly as she pushed her hips against his hardness, her panties pressed firmly against his boxers. Jake's lips once again found hers and his soft kisses caused her to moan in delight. With each moan, his hand slid further and further down her body until it reached the edge of her panties, and finally stopped at the small blue bow that adorned the top of her underwear.

Livi opened her eyes and looked intensely into Jake's green eyes. "It's okay," she whispered, anticipating what was coming. Jake smiled and kissed her softly and tenderly as his hand slid under her panties and caressed the excited area underneath. His fingers explored her, one minute gently rubbing her sweet spot and the next minute delving inside her with caressing movements that turned her moans into screams.

As he manipulated his fingers inside her, he began sucking her nipples, bringing her a happiness she had not known in a long time. Finally, just when she thought she could take no more, Livi exploded and she felt her butterflies leave her body, their wings gently tickling her upper thighs. As she lay there spent, Jake held her, kissing her forehead softly and whispering, "I love you."

When she finally came back down to earth, she realized Jake had not yet had the same liberating experience and she opened her eyes and looked at him. "Are you still . . . ?" Livi did not know how to ask this.

"I'm fine," Jake answered. "This is your time so just relax." He once again held her close and Livi no longer felt self-conscious of her body as she entwined her bare legs in his. He had seen or felt every inch of her and he still loved her. Life was good.

*

The next day at work, Livi's body felt like gelatin. She had experienced such a long dry spell as far as her sex life was concerned her body was not quite sure how to handle the past few days with Jake. She spent most of that day alone in her office, trying to keep her mind off him while catching up on what she missed at work the day before. She did not like things hanging over her head so it made her feel better to organize her workload and finish one task before moving on to the next.

Overall, it was a productive day and her busyness made the hours disappear on her watch. She wanted to escape at exactly five-o'clock again today and surprise Jake with dinner, so she was more than a little disappointed when Nadine appeared at her doorway at four-forty announcing that her boss, Robert, wanted to see her.

"Do you know what he wants?" Livi asked. She hoped he was not perturbed that she had taken Monday off.

"Have no idea. His assistant just said for you to come on up," said Nadine as she sat back down at her desk.

Livi grabbed her always-ready legal pad and pen and headed upstairs. She did not think this was promotion day because she still did not believe Robert was ready to leave yet after their discussion the other day. Maybe he just wanted to go over the Turnkitt closing. Maybe he had a new project for her. She really did not care the reason for the meeting as long as it was quick. Livi wanted to see Jake.

"Hey, sweetie," Robert's assistant said from her desk. "He said to go right in when you got here."

Livi opened the heavy mahogany door without knocking. There, sitting in *her* usual seat across from Robert's desk was Armani. Robert was somberly sitting behind his desk, but both men stood as she entered the large room.

"There she is," Robert motioned for Livi to come closer. "Livi, this is Edward Winston."

Edward Winston, formerly known as Armani to Livi, held out

his hand. "A pleasure to meet you, Olivia."

"Nice to meet you, too," said Livi. *Olivia? Why so formal?* she thought.

Robert motioned for both of them to sit so Livi sat, just not in her customary chair. She was a little put off by Edward taking her usual seat.

Robert began, "Livi, Edward is coming to work for Hampton Steel and I told him you could show him the ropes around here."

"Sure," Livi turned to Edward. "Whatever you need, I'll be happy to help. What department will you be working in?"

Robert answered, "Livi, Edward will be working in Legal."

Livi smiled at Edward. *Oh, my replacement!* she thought, *How very thoughtful of Robert.* Obviously, Robert wanted her to train Edward before he left so that Livi would not be overly burdened with that task when she moved up to general counsel.

Livi's brain started organizing her assigned task. "Great. When does he start?" she said to Robert.

"Yesterday," Edward replied without giving Robert time to blink.

"Wow," said Livi. Obviously her promotion was coming sooner than she thought and, for almost an instant, she regretted taking yesterday off with Jake. "Then we really need to get on the ball," she said.

Livi turned to Robert and continued, "I'll have Nadine print out a list of my open files along with a summary of their current status. Most are pretty much under control so it shouldn't take long for Edward to catch up. As for my office, I would think I can pack it up within a day or two so he can move in by the end of—"

"Livi," Robert interrupted. "Mr. Winston's office will be up on this floor. He. . .he is taking *my* place."

Immediately, all the air was sucked out of the room and Livi could not breathe. She felt like she was going to pass out. *What? Did I hear him right?* she thought. *Who is this guy that can just waltz in here and take all I have worked for?* Livi could not believe what was happening and struggled to keep her eyes focused without tearing up.

She gripped the arms of her chair as she looked at Robert and knew she would never forget the look on the old attorney's face. It was the look of defeat. As if he were an old dog chained in a junkyard who had been beaten down for the last time, vowing to never again attempt a jailbreak. She did not expect this look and for that reason it was stored in her memory bank forever. "I see," was all she could mutter, her white knuckles luckily being the only visible evidence of her distress.

Robert sat in silence and avoided her stare, knowing how much he had hurt her.

Edward's voice broke through their thoughts, saying, "Olivia, I'm sure we will make a great team and, in case I forget to tell you, thank you in advance for all your help in acclimating me to Hampton Steel."

"No problem." Livi spoke softly. "Whatever you need." She turned to Robert. "Is that all, sir? I have another appointment right now," she lied.

Edward answered her, "That's fine. We can deal with all this tomorrow."

Robert stared down at his desk without saying a word. It looked like he was being pushed into a corner by Edward without even putting up a fight. The proverbial torch had already been passed, and Livi was never in the race to begin with.

Livi stood up and got out of there as fast as she could without saying another word. She did not even acknowledge the good-bye from Robert's assistant. Feeling the tears finally pushing against her eyelids, she headed down the elevator, went straight to her office and grabbed her purse and coat, intentionally leaving her briefcase behind.

Nadine was not at her desk so Livi did not have to deal with her right now. She just wanted to get out of there and get to Jake. She left her office and hurried through the front lobby. Luckily, Barbara had already gone for the day, so she was not faced with any questions about her tears as she past the receptionist's desk.

She escaped to her car without seeing a soul and drove out of Hampton Steel's parking lot while trying to call Jake on her cell phone at the same time. She barely missed the parking lot exit and instead plowed over the curb, her car's undercarriage scraping the concrete just as Jake answered.

"Hey," Jake said, recognizing Livi's number by his cell phone's caller ID.

"Where are you?" Livi asked, her voice finally cracking.

"I'm at Nell's. What's wrong?" Jake asked.

"Can you meet me? I need you," Livi said, desperation dripping from her words. "How soon can you be at my house?"

"Right now," was all Jake had to say.

Chapter Nine

Jake held Livi while she cried out her disappointment on her living room sofa. Between tears, she tried to explain to him what just happened, that she lost her promotion to a stranger, that her boss, Robert Matthews, had unexpectedly kicked her in her gut and that her career was over without this promotion.

"Promotion" and "career" were not words required in Jake's vocabulary, so he had never put much thought into either of them. Nevertheless, he did not want to seem unsympathetic. He had never been in her shoes before, so he had no wise words to comfort her. Jake could only offer his arms around Livi and hope that would be enough for now.

Eventually Livi's tears stopped flowing and her disappointment transformed into anger. She stood up, back straight, and finally composed herself as she paced in the middle of her living room. When she saw Jake's shirt soaked through on his shoulder with her tears, she smiled sheepishly and said, "Sorry about your shirt. Let me get you a towel."

"No biggie. I don't need a towel. It will eventually dry . . . in a few months." Jake said as he tried to be funny. "Are you okay now?"

"I don't know. No," Livi replied honestly. She stood there staring out her home's front bay window.

"Well, what can we do to stop those tears, even if it is just for tonight?" Jake said. He had already moved into caretaker mode again.

"Probably nothing. This promotion was all I ever wanted. The past few years I have worked night and day for Hampton Steel, sacrificing any semblance of a normal life, all the while hoping I would move up when Robert retired. *I* was next in line! There *is* no one else! And out of nowhere comes this Mr. Winston, who obviously knows more about what's going on at Hampton Steel than I do!" Livi rambled. Her anger had finally erupted and, unfortunately for Jake, he was the only one there to witness it.

"Okay. Calm down. Let's not get that going again," Jake said. He did not know what to do with her so he took a shot at alcohol. "How about we go get a drink? We could hit DG's." DG's was the local pub, and Jake hoped a crowded karaoke night would buffer any more outbursts from Livi. Besides, karaoke always made her laugh in high school, and he had many fond memories of Livi acting silly on a microphone.

"I don't know if I am in the mood to go out. Are you sure you want to be seen with me like this?" Livi asked. She knew her eyes were red and puffy, and she did not think her eye cream would work fast enough to deflate them before she went out.

"You look beautiful to me." Jake meant what he said. He stood up and wrapped his strong arms around her as if to shield her from her own ugly thoughts and kissed her softly with the tenderness only a first love could experience.

*

Livi could not say "no" to Jake after that kiss so she quickly touched up her make-up and fed Gatsby his dinner. Her tears were still on the tips of her eyes, ready for takeoff again any second, but she tried valiantly to push thoughts of work aside for the night and concentrate on Jake. Her valiance did not succeed immediately, and she rode to DG's in the silence of Jake's truck, replaying today's meeting on the Executive Floor over and over again in her head. Livi's tears were still evident when Jake found a parking space near the bar, so the couple quickly headed inside for Livi's much-needed alcohol.

The Dry Goods Bar, or "DG's" as the locals called it, got its name from its location, a building formally home to the Miller and Sons Dry Goods store as evidenced by the faded sign painted on the bar's brick exterior. By all accounts it would be considered a dive in most cities, but in Millersville it was *the* place to have a drink and unwind.

The renovated building contained a large, saloon-type carved wooden bar, plenty of tables, a small dance floor for Friday's "Disco Night" and an even smaller stage for "Karaoke Tuesdays". Recognizing the mood she was in, Livi looked around and was grateful it was Tuesday and not Friday.

Despite its name, the only items sold at DG's that remotely resembled "dry goods" throughout the entire bar could be found on the menu, but the nachos, chicken fingers, cheese sticks and other pub food swam in grease so their "dryness" was highly questionable. The wine also had its own share of issues. Millersville rumor stated DG's white zinfandel was not really a zinfandel at all but instead a carefully crafted mixture of their house red and house white blended together to make the proper pink color of a white zinfandel. Other than that, the bar offered a variety of beers and liquors, and patrons were guaranteed their drink of choice, so long as their drink of choice was not white zinfandel.

Upon entering, Jake and Livi found a table perfectly positioned between the bar and the stage and just dark enough to hide Livi's puffy eyes. Jake ordered a pitcher of beer and the two sat closely together with their attention immediately directed to the sad soul on the stage who was attempting to channel Jon Bon Jovi with his version of "Desperado."

The man was obviously serious about his singing as his face contorted with each note and his grip on the microphone forced him to double over as if in pain. His seriousness did not translate into a decent singing voice, however, and Livi felt a little sorry for him. Someone should have told him a long time ago that he could not sing, but here he was, reliving his glory days as a garage band lead singer.

Jake leaned over and whispered in Livi's ear, "As my mother says, 'Bless his heart.'"

Livi laughed, realizing she and Jake were thinking the exact same thing about the pretend entertainer. Her laugh felt good and the beer began to work its magic. After the first pitcher and a half, as well as countless other fantasizing singers, the bar began to fill with its usual patrons who normally hit Karaoke Tuesday after dinner. Livi was feeling looser and was glad to see her sister and Todd enter and head over to their table. The young couple sat down just as Livi spotted Nell and her husband, Richard, at the bar buying drinks. The friends surrounded Livi and Jake's table and barged in to join them.

"I can't believe you are out tonight and not at work! Did you get fired?" Elizabeth joked.

Immediately Jake came to Livi's rescue. "There will be no talk about work tonight," Jake sternly instructed the table and he was obviously not joking. The firmness in his voice and the look on Livi's face dropped a hush over the friends.

"Did something happen?" Nell asked as she moved into her big sister mode.

"I didn't get the promotion," Livi could barely be heard over the karaoke singer but everyone got the picture.

"Oh Livi, I'm so sorry!" Elizabeth offered.

"How do you know?" Nell asked.

"Robert told me today. They gave the job to some guy named Winston," Livi said.

"Edward Winston?" asked Richard.

Livi nodded. "Do you know him?"

"No. Just heard the name lately. I had to run a bunch of reports the other day and send them to him. I assumed he was some outside accountant or something," said Richard.

"Nope, not an accountant. He's a lawyer and, as of yesterday, our new general counsel," Livi said as she stared into her beer and absently fingered the mug.

"Want me to run a background check on him? Maybe we could scoop up some dirt," joked Todd.

"No." Livi partially smiled, appreciating Todd's joke. "I'm sure Hampton Steel has already done that."

"Sorry, Liv. You would have been great in that position. But I'm sure it will be fine. Hampton Steel needs you," Richard said, trying to be reassuring. "I know what you need." He laughed and graciously took the microphone from the stage's latest victim.

"Nell, what is your husband doing?" Livi asked, more than a little shocked.

"You didn't know he was our local Karaoke King?" Nell said proudly.

Livi looked at Jake who shrugged his shoulders. Obviously this was news to him, too. All eyes turned to Richard who had a crazy grin under the stage lights.

Stepping on stage, Richard morphed into David Lee Roth as the opening to Van Halen's "Jump" began streaming from the karaoke speakers. He was still dressed in his dress shirt and tie from the office, but, despite his unforgiving work clothes, his movements mimicked the rock star.

"Livi!" Richard pointed to her from the stage and yelled, "This is for you because when life doesn't go the way you plan, you might as well jump!" And with that, Richard began singing the song's chorus while doing the best David Lee Roth jump his short, pudgy body could handle.

He looked silly but his antics accomplished their purpose, and Livi was soon laughing so hard she almost spewed beer all over Jake. The entire table erupted and, based on the response of the rest of the bar, it was evident that Richard was somewhat of a karaoke celebrity at DG's.

"Nell, he's fantastic!" Livi yelled. She could not believe her mild-mannered friend had so much rocker inside him.

"I know. He really is more entertaining than he lets on," replied Nell, looking around. "Have you seen Nadine yet? She's usually around here on Tuesdays."

"No. I haven't seen her tonight, but I haven't been looking for her either." Livi looked around but could not see anything. The bar was dark and filled to capacity so it was hard to make out faces in the crowd.

The night continued with more pitchers and karaoke from the close-knit group. Livi finally drank enough liquid courage to grace the stage with her own rendition of Aretha Franklin's "Respect" and her entire table cheered her on. When she stumbled forward as she tried to spell R-E-S-P-E-C-T while pointing her finger at the crowd, Jake knew it was time to take her home before someone got hurt. He met her as she staggered off the stage and then held her up as she said her good-byes to the group.

None of them had seen her like that in a long while, and all were happy the alcohol had done its job. Livi had not mentioned work in about four pitchers, and her glazed look and plastered smile assured her friends that work was out of her mind, at least until the next morning.

*

That night, Nadine sat in her apartment painting her toenails geisha red. She knew she was missing a good time at DG's, but she was sacrificing this Tuesday's fun for her master career plan.

Earlier that evening, she had worked later than usual and had missed Livi leaving the office. Nadine had been on one of her many bathroom primping breaks and had returned to find Armani instead of Livi in her boss's office. He had told Nadine he was looking for Olivia and then introduced himself as Edward Winston. Nadine had immediately smelled success and had flashed her bleached smile at the nice-looking stranger. She had remembered the way this stranger had looked at her in the lobby last week and Nadine was not going to let this flirting opportunity go to waste.

"I'm Nadine. It looks like Livi has already left for the day. Is there anything I can do to help?" Nadine had said, softening her voice to her best Marilyn Monroe sex tone.

"No. I can catch up with her tomorrow. I'm coming in to take Robert Matthews's place and just wanted to mention one more thing to Livi before I left tonight," Edward had said as he smiled at Nadine. He was obviously on the same teeth-whitening plan she was.

"Oh." This news had shocked Nadine but she had learned to maintain her composure in front of potential love interests, so she did not reveal her surprise to Edward. She had noticed he was wearing a wedding band but this fact rarely stopped Nadine once her sights were set. "I'll let her know you stopped by," Nadine said and again flashed her smile adding an eyelash bat for good measure.

"Thank you," Edward had said as he grabbed Nadine's hand with both of his and gave her the two-handed shake. "It was such a great pleasure meeting you." Edward had bent down, kissed Nadine's hand and left her office without another word. While other employees may have been taken aback, this unprofessional kiss had been an unexpected pleasure for Nadine.

As Nadine sat in her apartment that night, she replayed meeting Edward over and over again in her mind. She suddenly realized this dashing man could be worked into her master plan. She lay back on her couch waiting for her nails to dry and began visualizing different scenarios with Edward. *Yes, this could work out nicely*, thought Nadine as she settled into watching the Lifetime Channel on her big screen.

Chapter Ten

Edward Winston knew what he looked like driving to work and he liked his image. His Mercedes convertible stood out like a silver bullet in Millersville, and he only wished it was warm enough to put the top down so people could see him talking on his cell phone. He was superior to all the hicks in this town, so it would be easy to complete his plan here. He was saying just that very thing to the man on the other end of his cell phone that morning.

"Now don't get too cocky, Edward," the other man was saying. "These people may not be as stupid as you think they are. What about that Livi girl?"

"Don't worry about her. She reports to me now and, from what I hear, she values her job. She won't get in my way," Edward responded. *Besides,* thought Edward, *I've already hooked Livi's assistant.*

"Well, just remember what I said. Don't get cocky. That's what got you in trouble the last time," the other man said and abruptly hung up.

Don't get cocky, my ass, thought Edward, *I know what I'm doing.* Edward did not like being told what to do, but he knew how to take orders if taking orders got him what he wanted. Edward loved the power that came with his general counsel position at Hampton Steel because with that power came money.

For Edward, the two always came hand in hand and to obtain his power and the money that came with it, a certain image had to be upheld and Edward excelled at upholding images. He had his blonde trophy wife who luckily gave him twins, a boy and a girl, so he was not required to have any more children. He and his wife had replaced themselves in society, and now that his sperm donation was complete, the kids were his wife's problem, not his.

Although moving to Millersville was not his own choosing—

he could no longer live in New York thanks to the other man—it had been easy to find the best, gated community in which to keep up appearances. It was easy because Millersville only had one gated community, The Meadows, and most of the other Hampton Steel executives and board members lived there so obviously it was a necessity for Edward to live there as well. His children enrolled in the only private school Millersville had to offer, not because of the school's well-known academic excellence, but because having his children attend a private school fit Edward's image.

His wife had already joined the ladies' tennis group at the Millersville Country Club, and the thought of all those ladies in their tennis skirts hardened Edward's instrument as he turned into Hampton Steel's parking lot. At that moment, Edward decided that he had indeed set up his image nicely here in Millersville.

This will be a piece of cake, Edward thought as he parked his car in the executive lot. His space already had his nameplate, and he relished the fact it was in the front row where everyone at Hampton Steel could admire his car.

"Good morning, Mr. Winston. Congratulations and welcome to Hampton Steel," Barbara said, smiling as Edward walked through the lobby and past the receptionist's desk.

"Good morning, Barbara. You must have gotten the memo," replied Edward.

"Yes, sir. First thing this morning," Barbara said as Edward kept walking without any further acknowledgement of the receptionist.

He went straight to Livi's office and was surprised to find it empty.

"Livi's going to be a little late this morning," said Nadine as she entered her outer office from the hallway and sat down at her desk. "Is there anything I can do for you?" Nadine asked as she leaned over her desk toward Edward, pressing her arms together against her breasts so that their fullness extended up and over the top of her barely buttoned-up blouse. Nadine knew exactly what she was doing.

Edward could not help but stare. "No, I was just following up from last night. I wanted to give Olivia a heads up about a memo before it went out but I think I'm too late." Edward just kept staring at Nadine's breasts and she didn't seem to mind at all.

"I'll tell her to call you when she gets in. I don't think she was feeling well this morning so it may be ten o'clock or so before we see her. Is that okay?" asked Nadine. She leaned in even more. Her breasts looked as if they might just pop up out of her blouse.

"Oh, yeah. That is fine," said Edward, still looking at Nadine's breasts, and placing a double meaning to the phrase "that is fine." Nadine smiled as Edward exited her office with his still-hard instrument.

*

Livi woke that day and wondered how someone could have knit such little socks and placed them over each of her teeth while she slept. Her mouth was drier than dirt, and her head felt like it had been run over by a Mac Truck. Naturally, she vowed never to drink again and made her way to her bathroom where she found a note from Jake taped to the mirror: *Gotta go, love you, call you later—and good luck at work today.* Work. Livi's memory of her meeting with Edward and Robert was slowly returning.

No wonder she had gotten so drunk the night before. Livi called Nadine to let her assistant know she would be late and then began getting dressed. *What does one wear to her own execution?* Livi thought.

After taking a very long time to get dressed, Livi was finally in her car and heading to work. Upon her arrival, she immediately noticed Edward's car and nameplate in the executive parking lot. *And so it begins*, thought Livi. She headed straight through the lobby and past Barbara's desk. Barbara was on the phone but looked at Livi with sympathy and mouthed "sorry" to Livi as she walked past.

How does Barbara know? Livi thought. She continued on to her office and closed her door. Nadine was not at her desk and had probably taken the first of many primping runs today.

Livi wondered if Nadine knew of Livi's imminent demise. Her wondering did not last long as she saw the company memo announcing Edward's arrival sitting in her email inbox. She stared at it a very long time. Everyone knew by now that she had lost her promotion and Livi had no plan of action for dealing with this. Livi sat there staring until there was a knock on her door.

"Livi?" Nadine softly called.

Livi responded, "I'm here. Come on in." *Time to face this*, thought Livi. "I guess you heard," she said to Nadine, who was now standing in the open doorway.

"Yeah. Are you upset?" Nadine appeared to genuinely care.

"Yes. But we're not going to let the good ol' boys network know how upset, are we?" Livi asked as she tried to joke away her disappointment.

"No. You'll be fine. Just let me know if you need anything. And by the way, Edward already came by this morning looking for you," Nadine said, and she turned to sit back down at her desk. She did feel a little sorry for Livi, but she could not let a high school friendship get in the way of her master plan. Nadine needed Edward more than she needed Livi now.

Edward? thought Livi. *One memo and Nadine is already on a first name basis with this guy?* Livi's bitterness was not going away today. She tasted it on the tip of her tongue as she yelled into Nadine's outer office, "Well, find Mr. Edward Winston and tell him I'm here if he wants to see me now."

As Nadine called around looking for Edward, Livi's cell phone rang. She saw it was her father but decided not to answer. She knew Elizabeth had told him about her downfall at work, so he was worried about her. However, she did not have the energy or ability to reassure him right now. She would deal with her father later.

Edward appeared in Livi's office a few minutes later, but Livi chose not to shake his hand when he entered. She was normally wary of strangers and would make no exception even if he was her boss.

"Olivia, I just wanted to give you a heads up about a memo before you got here this morning. I know it is a little late now," Edward said and flashed his smile at Livi.

Livi did not smile back. "Thanks," she said. "Obviously, I did not expect such a memo to go out to the entire company before I had time to tell my staff." No one could have ignored Livi's coolness.

"Well, maybe we can catch up later on today. I would like to see those files you mentioned yesterday," Edward said, still smiling.

"Of course. Just let me know," Livi responded. Her coolness was expanding throughout the room.

Edward recognized that his smiles and charm were not working on Livi. "I'll get with Nadine to set up a time for us to meet," said Edward as he quickly exited her office. Edward headed straight to his office, closed the door, and dialed the other man on his cell phone.

"Yes?" the other man answered.

"You were right about Livi. I don't think we can count on her. But don't worry, her assistant will make a nice substitute and she doesn't look half bad, either," Edward said. He was pleased with himself for being able to solve his problem so quickly.

"Look." The other man sounded stern. "Just keep your eye on the ball here. Don't let your sex drive get in the way—again. I mean it this time. This is an all or nothing deal and the sooner it is over, the sooner we're on our way to the Caymans. Got it?"

"Yes, sir," said Edward, still hard with his thoughts of Nadine.

Chapter Eleven

Livi stared at the engraved printed invitation Hampton Steel's mailroom just hand-delivered to her office and tried to figure a way out of going. It had only been a week since Edward started working at the company but Hampton Steel's board of directors had already planned a cocktail party this upcoming weekend in order to welcome the allegedly bright new attorney into the Hampton Steel family.

For Livi, however, this weekend was not convenient. Edward had been piling on the work so she had not seen Jake since Karaoke Tuesday. Livi had hoped she and Jake could make up for lost time this weekend and, while the invitation said she could bring a guest, she did not want their lost time to be made up at some stuffy Hampton Steel function for Edward.

Her butterflies needed Jake and they did not want to go to the party either. So there she sat, trying to dodge her new boss's celebratory party without committing professional suicide.

In her one week working for Edward, Livi had decided she did not like him. She could not pinpoint an exact reason. She just knew he rubbed her the wrong way. Maybe it was the charming sleaziness he exuded when he flirted with the office staff. Maybe it was the way he always called her "Olivia." Maybe it was because she did not know anything about him, and here he was, in total control of her career. Whatever the reason, Livi did not like her new boss.

The only reason Livi could come up with for attending the soiree was to see Robert Matthews. She had not seen or heard from her former boss since their fateful meeting in his office, and it hurt her that Robert did not have the guts to face her. With all their years working together, she felt he could at least tell her why Edward had gotten the job instead of her.

It certainly could not have been Edward's taste. The slime ball had already moved into Robert's office and tackied it up with modern knick-knacks. Deep down, Livi missed Robert and the class he had conveyed over Hampton Steel's Executive Floor, as well as its board of directors. Even drunk, her former boss had more grace than Edward would ever have in his ring-encircled pinkie, and Livi knew she would miss Robert's southern elegance permeating Hampton Steel's work atmosphere.

In the end, Livi knew she had to attend the party despite the fact that she was more than a little nervous about it. This would be the first time she would see all of Hampton Steel's upper management together since she lost her promotion to Edward. She assumed everyone except she knew the reason she had been passed over for the general counsel's position and facing them was going to be beyond awful, but her pride would not let her hide.

Besides, Jake had promised Livi he would stick by her side all night and, while Jake was less than enthusiastic about the situation, Livi thought that, deep down, Jake was looking forward to meeting the infamous Edward. Livi had previously assured Jake that he could take Edward out with one punch of his fist, and this small bit of information had boosted Jake's ego enough that he had agreed to being the dutiful beau at her company function. Despite the ego boost, however, Livi knew that Jake secretly hoped the night would pass quickly so the two of them could eventually have some alone time.

*

"Wow," was all Jake said when he picked her up for the party, and Livi immediately knew her little black dress had been the perfect choice for the evening. Jake was actually wearing a suit, but he constantly tugged at his neck unknowingly, as if his tie were choking him.

"Wow, right back," replied Livi. Jake looked good and strong and Livi's evil side imagined him actually decking Edward with one swift blow.

"Where is this thing, anyway?" asked Jake as he opened the truck door for Livi.

"In The Meadows at Joseph Sullivan's home," Livi replied. Mr. Sullivan was one of the older and wiser members of Hampton Steel's board of directors. He was one of Robert's few allies on the board and usually voted on the side of the general counsel. He had always been kind to Livi, so she was glad this insufferable night would take place in a friend's home. At least she would know where the bathrooms were when her nervous nausea caused her to throw up all over the party.

They arrived at The Meadows entrance gate and, after indicating they were there to see Mr. Sullivan, were motioned inside by the night guard. They soon arrived at their destination, which was more a mansion than a home. The massive brick exterior, tall stone columns and floor-to-ceiling windows rose up out of the ground as part of the landscape bordering The Meadows golf course.

The plentiful cars parked in front of the mansion indicated the party was already in full swing and Livi was fine with that. Perhaps they could sneak in, make the obligatory small talk with Mr. Sullivan and Edward, and then sneak back out without seeing the rest of the Hampton Steel management team. *Wishful thinking*, thought Livi.

Jake and Livi walked the long driveway, holding hands in silence. When they reached the massive wooden front door, Jake rang the doorbell and Livi took a deep breath. Mrs. Sullivan answered the door and gave Livi the obligatory welcoming hug. *So far, so good*, thought Livi. After speaking with Mrs. Sullivan for a short while, Livi led Jake to the bar in the living room for some much needed liquid courage.

"Let's not repeat Karaoke Tuesday here," whispered Jake with a warning smile.

"No problem. I hope we're not here long enough to have that chance." Livi smiled back and sipped her wine. Across the room, Livi spied Robert Mathews sitting in a massive wing-backed chair near the fireplace. She started toward him but, as she got closer, his eyes revealed that he had started partying long before he arrived at the Sullivans' that night.

He spotted Livi and smiled his drunken smile, but then his glassy eyes roamed away from her. It was obvious that her presence did not register in his Dewar's scotch-saturated mind. Livi realized she was not getting any answers from her former boss tonight, at least none she could understand, so she decided to shelve her questions for another day.

"Well, there she is! Ms. Olivia!" Edward's voice rose up behind her like fingernails on a chalkboard.

Livi turned to face her new boss and said with sweet venom, "Hello, Edward."

"I see you've already found the bar." Edward leaned in and whispered, "And so has Robert." Edward pointed to the former general counsel and rolled his eyes as if he and Livi were in on some private joke.

"I'm sure he will be fine," said Livi as she leaned away out of reach of Edward's merlot-tinged breath and grabbed Jake's arm to pull him close to her. "Edward, this is Jake Cooper."

"Nice to meet you," said Jake, grabbing Edward's hand and giving it a firm, hard shake.

"You too." Edward looked up at him, seeming impressed by Jake's strength. "So Livi, were you able to finish closing out the Turnkitt file like I asked?" Edward said in an obvious attempt to establish his dominance over Livi in front of her date.

"I should have it to you by Monday morning," Livi replied with a smile. *What a jerk*, she thought.

"Great," Edward responded but he did not sound like he was really very interested in the Turnkitt file. At that moment, a tall, pale, very thin, blonde woman slinked up to Edward and put her arm through his.

"Dah-ling," the thin woman purred. "I just got a call from the babysitter and Ward is not feeling well so I must head home. I know you probably need to stay, so do you mind if I take the car? I'm sure you can catch a ride home with someone since it is just down the street. Is that all right?"

Images of Cat Woman from *Batman* flashed in Livi's mind.

"Of course, my love," Edward said. He seemed almost pleased that his child was sick, "Oh, and call me later and let me know what's going on with the twin." With that, the tall, pale, very thin, blonde woman slinked back out of the room.

"Was that your wife?" asked Livi.

"Oh, I should have introduced you! Yes, that's my wife. She was a little nervous about leaving the twins tonight, new babysitter and all. I'm sure the kid's okay." Edward leaned in again to whisper, "Probably using the kid as an excuse to leave the party. She doesn't like these company functions very much."

Livi once again confirmed she did not like this man. *His children obviously have names,* she thought, *but to him they are just "the twins."*

"Well, better go mingle some more," Edward suggested. With that, he turned to his next conversation target, Hampton Steel's CFO.

"I guess he can mark us off his list now. Maybe we won't have to talk to Edward any more tonight," Jake said. He actually sounded hopeful.

"Sounds good to me," said Livi, finishing off her glass of wine. She glanced around the room and was surprised to see Nadine standing at the bar. She, too, was wearing a little black dress. However, Nadine's definition of "little" was considerably shorter than Livi's. Nadine spotted Livi and Jake and quickly made her way over to them.

"Well, hey stranger," Nadine said to Jake as she gave him a hug that lasted longer than it should have.

"Hey, Nadine. I hear you are keeping Livi straight now," joked Jake.

"I don't know about that," Nadine blushed and batted her eyes at Jake. She then turned to Livi and gushed, "Isn't this a great party, Liv? It was so nice of the board to invite the whole legal department!"

"I guess," Livi replied. *How could Nadine be so cavalier about this party?* Livi thought. *It's for Edward after all.*

"Have you seen the food? The shrimp are huge!" Nadine squealed. She acted as if she had never seen shrimp before. "I'm going back for more." And with that she flitted toward the formal dining room.

"She's having fun," offered Jake.

"She always does," said Livi.

Livi's wine was helping and she was on her second glass when she finally spotted the mansion's owner and her host for the evening. One short tête-à-tête with him and she and Jake were out of there. Joseph Sullivan was standing in a corner by himself and appeared to be surveying the party and his guests like a grandfather at a family reunion. He was a tall, thin man with a full head of hair. He was distinguished, and his eyes revealed the wisdom that accompanied his aging years.

Despite that, he looked alone in that corner. Not lonely, as if he was desperate to find a friend, but alone, as if he had looked but there were no friends to be found. His look almost made Livi want to stay with him longer than the intended short tête-à-tête as she made her way through the crowded room toward the elder gentleman.

"Hello, Mr. Sullivan," Livi said, "This is a lovely party. Thank you for having us."

"Livi! Always a pleasure to have you in our home," Mr. Sullivan exclaimed. He seemed happy to see her but slightly distracted. "And Jake, good to see you. How are your parents?"

"Fine, Mr. Sullivan. I'll tell them you said hello," Jake responded as he shook his host's hand.

"You do that. So are you two having a good time?" asked Mr. Sullivan.

"Yes, of course," Livi replied. "But we have to go soon so I just wanted to thank you and your wife for having us."

"No problem. If I have to do this, I might as well enjoy my friends here," Mr. Sullivan said as he put an arm around Livi. "How are you holding up dear?" he whispered.

"Fine," Livi whispered back, but she allowed her eyes to reveal more as she looked at Mr. Sullivan. She looked over to Jake who appeared to realize that he was not invited to this portion of the conversation. Jake said his good-byes and left the party to pull his truck up to the front door.

"Look, Livi, nothing ever stays the same. I've had to come to grips with that recently," Joseph Sullivan spoke to her like a teacher to a student. "This is all happening so fast but you are a sharp girl. I know you will be fine. It's the rest of the town I am worried about. Edward and his buddy are selfish. They only think of themselves. They don't realize how this will affect families, other businesses in Millersville. The whole town will be devastated. It truly is sad when the moral minority consists of an old geezer like me and a drunk," Mr. Sullivan said as he pointed to Robert, now officially passed out in the same winged-back chair. Mr. Sullivan, at this moment, seemed to be musing more to himself than to Livi, who had no clue what the old man was talking about.

"Sir?" Livi whispered to Mr. Sullivan, almost as if to remind him that she was standing there.

"Oh," Mr. Sullivan was pulled back into the two-party conversation. He looked down and smiled at Livi, but it was either a sad smile or a fake smile. Livi could not tell which.

"Sir, I'm not sure what you are talking about," she said.

"Oh, don't pay any attention to me. I'm just a rambling old sentimental fool. You better go now. I'm sure Mr. Cooper is waiting," Mr. Sullivan paused and then leaned down to whisper in her ear, "But Livi, promise me you will be careful when dealing with your new boss. I am not sure I trust him just yet."

"Uh, sure, but. . ." Livi was confused, but her confusion would not be alleviated tonight because at that moment Joseph Sullivan abruptly turned to make his way over to Robert who obviously needed his friend's help right now.

The whole town will be devastated. Livi was left standing in that corner not understanding at all what just happened. She eventually turned to make her way to the front door where Jake's truck was waiting outside and, as she passed through the mansion's foyer, she spotted Nadine and Edward huddled together talking in the dining room.

Nadine was obviously in flirt mode, something Livi had seen before, but the characters in this particular scene only added to her confusion. Her assumedly loyal assistant, conspiring with the enemy? Livi felt like she was in the middle of a carnival fun house and needed to get out of there fast.

As usual, Jake was there to open Livi's door but his chivalry did not take her mind away from her confusion.

"What's wrong?" he asked.

"Just thinking," she replied.

"About what?"

"Edward," said Livi.

They rode the rest of the way home in silence.

*

Edward meeting Nadine in the Sullivan dining room that night was leading to more than a flirtatious episode between the ambitious Hampton Steel coworkers.

"I appreciate the ride home," Edward said as he sat in Nadine's car after the Sullivan party. "Do you want to get a drink before you drop me off?"

"Sure." Nadine knew where this night was heading, and she loved it when a plan came together. She had left the party first and waited in her car for almost twenty minutes before Edward discreetly slid into the passenger's seat of her coupe. They were both adults with their own agendas, so Nadine knew what she was getting into when Edward had asked her for a ride home earlier that evening.

They both appeared to be on the same page and she loved that each could still feign innocence enough to fake morality. Getting a drink was the logical next step in her plan. "My apartment is close by. We could just go there," offered Nadine.

"Sounds good." Edward leaned back and draped his arm over the back of Nadine's seat.

Nadine lived in the most upscale apartment complex that small town Millersville had to offer, and it maintained its exclusivity by being located near The Meadows gated community. The ride was short and Nadine soon parked in her designated space near the elevator in the complex's underground garage. They rode the elevator in silence with Nadine standing slightly in front of Edward so that he could get a good look at her perfectly shaped posterior. She had played this game a hundred times and knew exactly where to stand in this elevator so that her features had the best light. Even though she was somewhat of a pro at riding the elevator under these circumstances, tonight she felt unusually nervous in the presence of Edward's power, and Nadine was glad he could not see her face right now.

*

The elevator stopped and Nadine led Edward to her apartment door. He watched her walk and knew he was not with the typical naïve secretary he was used to. This girl was special, and her confidence intoxicated Edward. This intoxication guided Edward's next move as Nadine unlocked her front door. He knew they were not really there to get a drink and he did not feel like wasting any more time.

She opened the door and before she knew what was happening, Edward slammed the door behind him and spun Nadine around, pushing her up against the foyer wall. They stared into each other's eyes, breaths rapid and heavy with anticipation. Neither said a word, but their eyes revealed a mutual knowledge that no one expected to make love that night. No, instead they were going to have sex. Rough, insensitive, selfish sex. The kind of sex only two egomaniacs with ulterior motives could experience together.

*

The lack of pretense excited Nadine. Normally, her small town sexual conquests required her to at least make an effort at innocence, thereby allowing them to return to their wives or girlfriends with a little less guilt. But Edward was different, and Nadine felt it in the rough way he pinned her against the wall. Not to be outdone, Nadine ripped open his shirt, his buttons popping off like champagne corks. She buried her lips in his chest, then moved up his neck until she found his ear. Nadine nibbled hard and whispered, "You are definitely my kind of man."

"You have no idea," Edward rasped as he pushed Nadine's little black dress up over her hips.

Chapter Twelve

The whole town will be devastated. . .Promise me you will be careful when dealing with your new boss.

These words swirled and burned in Livi's brain and she was now unable to think of anything else. While she had been able to spend time with Jake the previous weekend, Mr. Sullivan's distracting words had diminished the romantic mood created by Jake's reappearance in her life, so she had not felt her butterflies at all recently. Whereas a few weeks ago, all her thoughts centered on Jake, now she sat at her desk obsessing over a man in an entirely different way. *Promise me you will be careful when dealing with your new boss.*

What in the world did Mr. Sullivan mean by that? Be careful? Then she suddenly thought, *Is my job in jeopardy?* The thought of losing her job jolted Livi. She never imagined doing anything else but working for Hampton Steel, so this sudden realization actually made her sit straight up in her desk chair as if someone had just stuck a pin in her back. She needed to find out more about Mr. Winston but she did not know where to start.

Livi left her office and decided to walk the halls. She needed to think, and walking the halls would get her away from her phone and computer. She occasionally did this when stuck on any number of random legal issues of the day, so it was not unusual to see her walking around Hampton Steel with a contemplative look on her face.

But today she was lost in her thoughts of Edward when she passed the suite of offices that made up Hampton Steel's human resource department. As if her passing this department was a sign, Livi decided this would be a good place to start. She entered the suite and approached a secretary who also acted as the receptionist for the department.

"Hello." Livi was surprised she felt so nervous.

The secretary looked up from her desk in the middle of the room. "Well, hello Ms. Miller. What brings you down our way?"

Livi was not sure how to ask about Edward without appearing jealous or nosy. "Uh, I was wondering. . ." Livi hesitated, hoping an excuse would come to her. "I was wondering if you know, um. . ." And then it came to her. "If you know where Mr. Winston is licensed to practice law? In what state is Mr. Winston licensed? You see, uh, I keep track of, um. . . where all our attorneys are licensed and I need to add him to our database. I would ask him myself, but I can't seem to find him right now so I thought your department could help me." Livi knew she was rambling but did not care if it got the ball rolling with this secretary.

"Mr. Winston? I have no idea. We haven't even set up a file on him yet. We don't have anything to put in it." The secretary shrugged her shoulders.

"No file? What about his application, his background check? Do we not have a copy of his law license?" Livi asked, flabbergasted by this breach of procedure.

"Nope. Mr. Chamberlain from the board of directors just told us he was here to take Mr. Matthews's place and that he would get us the paperwork later. I know it sounds funny but we assumed it would be okay since it came from the chairman of the board. Is that a problem?" the secretary said, not knowing how helpful she was being.

"Problem? No, of course not, if it came from Mr. Chamberlain," Livi said as she smiled.

"Sorry we can't help. Try payroll. Mr. Winston must be set up with them if he wants to be paid. They may know something about his law license," said the secretary.

"Thanks," said Livi and she immediately headed to payroll. At least now she better understood why she had not gotten the job. Alexander Chamberlain had been chairman of Hampton Steel's board of directors for as long as she could remember and, according to the company rumor mill, he had fought with Robert Matthews every single day of his tenure.

Mr. Chamberlain did not like Robert and thus, guilty by association, the chairman did not like Livi. If he were the leader of the pack finding Robert's replacement, she never had a chance to begin with. She now understood Robert's look the day he had introduced her to Edward. Robert had fought his final battle with Chamberlain and he had lost. He had lost his final battle over Livi, and she felt sorry for Robert more than ever.

She took the elevator up to accounting and headed for the payroll manager. As she got closer to the payroll department, she could hear Edward's voice booming from the manager's office and she knew her opportunity for questions today was already lost. Edward apparently had gotten his claws in the manager because both men sounded like two fraternity brothers hooting and hollering behind the closed door.

The payroll manager was part of Hampton Steel's underground good old boys network, so Livi usually tried to steer clear of him. If he were in his office bonding with Edward, she would not get any answers from payroll today, and perhaps not ever.

Frustrated, Livi headed back down to her office. Livi's Type A personality did not allow any questions to go unanswered for long and Mr. Sullivan's words kept beating her brain like a drum: *Promise me you will be careful when dealing with your new boss.* Usually when faced with a problem, she could eventually figure out the steps to resolve it. But her problem of Edward was different. She had to be discreet when looking into her new boss or she would definitely lose her job. Livi eventually reached her floor and, lost in her thoughts, she passed through Nadine's office without saying a word.

"Hey," Nadine said, sitting at her desk. "Wake up. I've got messages for you."

"Sorry," said Livi as she returned to Nadine's desk. "I'm just a little distracted today."

"Well, you better come back to earth because Edward left a bunch of files on your desk while you were out. He wants you to call him about them. Also, Jake called."

"Thanks," said Livi as she headed to her office. Nadine was not exaggerating when she referred to the files on Livi's desk as a "bunch." The pile was huge and Livi began looking through them for a clue as to why they were on her desk. They contained the Turnkitt financials and really belonged in the finance department. Livi picked up the phone and called Edward's assistant.

"Nadine said you wanted me to call you," Livi said when she finally reached her new boss.

"Yes, Olivia. I left some files on your desk. I was hoping you could rummage through them and organize them for a presentation I am giving to the board."

"But I thought I was presenting the Turnkitt closing to the board." Livi was incredulous. She had worked this deal and, now that it was finally closed, Edward was going to take the glory to Hampton Steel's board of directors. *How could he!* she thought, anger now oozing from every pore.

"I know this was your deal, but Mr. Chamberlain thought it would be better if I presented it to the board," Edward said. He knew name-dropping would get him what he wanted here.

"Of course," Livi responded, "but shouldn't these files belong in finance? Shouldn't someone there organize these numbers for *your* presentation?" She unsuccessfully tried to calm herself.

"No. I really want you to do it," Edward replied without giving any further explanation. He was her boss. He did not need to give her any other explanation.

"Okay. And you want it when?" Livi said in a tone her mother would not have approved of. She could not believe this man's arrogance.

"First thing tomorrow morning. Sound good?" Edward said. He knew this was virtually impossible. It would take at least two days to get through these files.

"Absolutely," Livi said firmly and hung up. She was not about to let this man win. She looked down at her phone and remembered she needed to call Jake.

"Hey, gorgeous." Jake answered his phone on the first ring.

"Hey. Bad news. I need to work late tonight so I don't think I can make dinner," Livi said. She and her butterflies were very disappointed.

"Damn. I really want to see you. What if I brought you dinner and we ate at your desk?" Jake asked. He was clearly disappointed, also.

"No. I don't even have time for that. Edward has really piled it on and I need to meet his deadline of tomorrow morning. It looks like I will be pulling an all-nighter. Can I take a rain check on dinner?" Livi responded.

"Sure." Jake paused. "And, hey, while you are in the middle of all that important work at two in the morning. . ."

"Yes?" Livi said.

"Just remember I love you," said Jake.

"I love you, too," said Livi as she hung up the phone. She resented Edward even more for taking her away from Jake again, but she also knew she was not in the mind set to tackle the files just yet. So, without thinking, she sat down at her computer and typed "Edward Winston" into Google. At least that was a start.

Chapter Thirteen

"Look. I told you I have it under control!" Edward roared. He was practically screaming into his cell phone. Luckily, he was the only person in the car.

"I don't care what you've *told* me! You are the only one who can handle this Livi girl so you better handle her!" The other man was screaming, also. "She obviously has an issue with you. Why else would she search for your name on the Internet? Thank goodness that girl was stupid enough to use Hampton Steel's computer for the search. How much did you have to pay that IT guy?"

In an attempt to sound calmer, Edward took a deep breath and replied, "It does not matter how much. What's done is done. We are monitoring her computer so I can keep a closer eye on her. Besides, I'm piling so much busy work on her she won't have time to even type my initials on her keyboard. I've got it covered, okay?"

"You better," said the other man as he abruptly hung up.

*

Livi felt like crap. She had just hung up the phone with Jake, who was obviously losing his patience with her. She had broken her fourth date in a row with him due to one of Edward's random document requests, and Jake was less than understanding of her work situation. He had actually told her she was "obsessed with Edward."

"I am not!" she had said, in self-defense.

"Yes, you are!" Jake had replied. "You are working night and day to meet his ridiculous deadlines and, on top of that, you think he is out to get you. Did you ever think he just has a different management style than Robert?" Jake had seemed tired of reasoning with Livi. "Look, I'm not defending the guy. I think he is a slimy jerk. But you need to get your priorities straight and tell this guy you have a life outside work!"

"I know. You are right. Just let me finish these last few projects. Then we can catch up this weekend. We can still go horseback-riding Saturday morning, can't we?"

"Sure. See you then," Jake had said in a tone Livi had not heard since her first semester in college.

Livi sat at her desk staring at the document on her computer. Jake should understand her predicament. This was her career, her life. She just needed time to get a handle on the situation with Edward, then she could concentrate wholeheartedly on her relationship with Jake. Gatsby understood her work ethic—of course, he had a doggie door and self-feeder so he did not need much more than that from her. Livi just wanted Jake to be as understanding as her dog.

As soon as she deciphered Mr. Sullivan's cryptic warning, Livi and her butterflies would make everything up to Jake, so his frustration with her now forced even more urgency into her research on Edward.

Livi's Google search had not provided her much information. All she found was Edward's prior address in upstate New York and the realtor who sold his previous home. She glanced at the Post-It note with the address and realtor's number and decided to give it a shot. She closed the door to her office, noting that Nadine was not at her desk, again. Lately, her assistant had been absent from her desk more than usual, and Livi assumed the number of her primping breaks had increased for some odd reason that Livi really did not care enough about right now. Livi sat behind her desk and dialed the realtor.

"Hello," a lady with a heavy New York accent answered.

"Hi. I saw a house listed on your website a while back but now it is not there. If I give you the address, could you tell me if it sold or not?" Livi asked. She was getting good at faking detective.

"Sure," the lady answered. "What's the address?"

"505 Pembroke." Livi fingered the Post-It note.

"Well, that was my listing! Yes, dear, I'm afraid it already sold," the lady said as she perked up, proud to flaunt her sale.

"Oh, that's too bad," Livi responded. She was running out of excuses to talk to the realtor. "Do all your sales go through that fast?"

"Well, we try. We had a very eager seller in this instance. His father had gotten him a job down south somewhere and he needed to hurry up and get down there. He took the first offer he received. Now, that doesn't happen too often," the realtor gossiped.

"I'm sure it doesn't," Livi said. "Well, thank you anyway."

"Can I interest you in anything else?" the now zealous sales lady continued. She was not going to let Livi off the phone that easily.

"Not today, but thank you. I'll call you after I look around some more," Livi said and quickly hung up. *So, Edward's father knows Chamberlain.* That explained a lot. These were baby steps but she was slowly getting Edward's story. Livi looked at the document on her computer screen.

She needed to forget Edward for now and get back to work if she was going to see Jake this weekend. The thought of a weekend with Jake caused her butterflies to skip a little, and this movement of her butterflies was just what she needed to leave her research on Edward and focus her concentration on the document in front of her.

*

Nadine was practically giddy with anticipation. She and Edward had worked out a code whereby he could signal her for clandestine meetings in his office. So far, their system had worked without anyone catching on. Livi had too much work now to know what was going on outside her own office, and Edward made sure Livi's new projects did not involve her assistant.

Nadine was clever enough to enter Edward's office without his secretary seeing her and so, here she was this afternoon, leaning back against Edward's desk, awaiting his arrival. Sneaking around the office made sex so much more exciting for Nadine. She had always thought office sex was taboo because it would have placed her job in jeopardy. But she did not have this concern with Edward. Nadine thought she knew all his secrets so, in her opinion, office sex with Edward only increased Nadine's job security.

Finally, Edward entered his office to find Nadine looking like a puppy begging for a bone. The minute he closed the door behind him, Nadine sat on top of his desk and spread her legs apart, forcing her short skirt to ride up her hips and revealing the fact that she was not wearing any underwear.

"That is a nice surprise," Edward said, pointing to the naked area between Nadine's legs.

"Do you like that? I thought it would save us some time from now on." Nadine was in manipulation mode.

"You are so efficient," said Edward as he locked his office door and headed toward her.

"Of course, I am. Come here and let me show you how efficient," said Nadine as she wrapped her long legs around Edward's hips and pulled him toward her. He sleazily smiled down at Nadine as his hands roughly grabbed at her breasts.

"Man, you are good," said Edward. He glanced down at her fullness in the palms of his hands and said, "I can't believe a woman like you exists in this hick town."

"I exist, but I'm not in this hick town for long. Remember your promise about the Caymans?" purred Nadine as she pushed her chest out so Edward could get a better grasp of her breasts. She knew she was good at playing the sex game and used it to her full advantage with Edward.

"I can't wait. Just you, me and time on our hands. Whatever will we do?" Edward whispered in Nadine's ear as he laid her back on the desk and spread her legs apart even more, revealing the one thing other than money that Edward could no longer resist.

Chapter Fourteen

The sunrise at the farm had been beautiful that Saturday morning and Jake wished Livi had been there to see it with him. The gold, orange and pink of the sky had mixed with the yellow and red of the fall trees and the entire landscape had looked like God's fireplace.

It was the kind of morning that surprisingly made Jake yearn to stay in Millersville for the rest of his life. He just wished Livi could experience his feeling of finally being settled, to see what her life could be like outside work if she just gave their relationship a real chance. Lately, however, he had felt like he was the only one committed to their togetherness, and he was really counting on today to get the two of them back on track together.

Livi had to work late the night before but had promised to meet him at his stable by eight o'clock that morning. The stable was rebuilt two years ago with new concrete floors and beautiful beamed ceilings. There was still a newness to the stable aromas and even the hay smelled more clean than musty.

Jake was anxious to see Livi and hoped to arrange a romantic tryst in one of these clean, hay-filled stalls later that day. Eight o'clock eventually came and went and the horses began to get restless. Wanting to be ready at exactly eight o'clock, Jake had already saddled them and strapped on a picnic basket filled with Livi's favorite food. The horses knew they were ready to go and did not like standing there without any riders. Jake was growing impatient as well and finally called Livi when the clock in the stable office showed the time to be eight-thirty-five.

"Hello," Livi groggily answered after quite a few rings. Jake had obviously woken her up.

"Hey. Are you coming?" he asked.

"Oh, my gosh! What time is it?" Livi asked. She was waking up now.

"Eight thirty-five. You were supposed to be here thirty-five minutes ago," Jake responded not too happily. His impatience was turning into anger as he realized she had simply overslept. Punctuality was important to Jake and he felt this was an indication where he fell on Livi's priority list.

"Oh, Jake! I am so sorry," Livi said. "I must have overslept. I worked all night at the office and just got home a little while ago. I thought I had time for a quick nap, but I must have slept right through the alarm. Could I meet you this afternoon? That way I can get a little shut-eye before we go for a ride."

"No," was all Jake said.

"What do you mean 'No'?" asked Livi.

"I mean 'No,'" said Jake matter-of-factly. "I am sick and tired of playing second fiddle to your office. We have had today planned for weeks and you know it. I'm not going to rearrange my day so you can *try* to fit me into your schedule. I'm sorry Livi, but I'm just not going to do it. Now, are you coming right now or not?" Jake asked in a huff.

"Jake! I said I was sorry. What more do you want me to do?" she exclaimed.

"I want you to put me first. Not work. Me!" Jake's anger erupted. He was holding his phone so tightly it almost broke into two pieces.

"Jake, please understand. I'm trying to hang on to what is left of my career and just need a little patience from you right now, that's all," pleaded Livi.

"Livi, I have been patient. Do you know how long it has been since we've been together? Too long!" Jake yelled. He let loose his anger in full throttle. "It's me or work. Choose. Now!"

"Jake!" Livi yelled right back at him. "You know I have a lot to deal with right now with Edward and Hampton Steel. Besides, I am not your mother. I can't stay home all day waiting for you to come off the fields like your father did. My work is important to me and you need to understand that."

Jake could not believe this was happening again. Livi might as well be sitting in her dorm at the University of Virginia. It was essentially the same discussion all over again.

"Look, Livi," Jake said as he tried to calm himself down. "I have tried to be understanding but this isn't working. We obviously have different priorities here. I know work is important to you, but I want a woman who puts me first. Can *you* understand that?"

Jake could not believe what he was saying. He was already in too deep and the thought of losing Livi was killing him. Jake was hoping he could force her to see his side in this situation.

"I see," Livi said softly. "I guess we are in two different places."

"So that's it, then?" Jake asked. His heart was pounding through his chest.

"I guess so," Livi responded heavily.

"Okay," Jake said as he realized what was really happening. "Uh, still friends, right?"

"Sure," choked Livi. She sounded like she was crying. "See you around."

"Yeah," Jake said and hung up. He sat down in a stall, angry beyond belief. How could she have done this to him a second time? He was so mad at her for being selfish but madder still at himself for getting sucked in again. He sat in that hay-filled stall for a good thirty minutes before he composed himself enough to unsaddle the horses. When that chore was finished, he headed to the guesthouse.

His eyes were red with despondency, and he knew exactly what he needed. He needed a drink. He needed his eyes to be red like a drunk who lives near the town's only liquor store, not like some sap who just lost the love of his life for the second time around.

Jake found his bottle of Jack Daniels in the top cabinet above the refrigerator and headed to the back porch of the guesthouse. He was due for a good binge, and the bourbon felt smooth sliding down his throat. He did not care what time of the morning it was. He would drink until he passed out. That way he could not think about her.

Chapter Fifteen

If people thought Livi was a workaholic before, they would consider her psychotic now. The devastation of losing Jake for the second time forced Livi to immerse herself in her work and in her quest to discover the real Edward with an even greater intensity. She spent all weekend crying to the point of dehydration, but by Monday morning she was ready to lose herself in her work at Hampton Steel.

Her sister and father had been taking turns calling her each hour on the hour all weekend long, but Livi kept assuring them she was fine. She really did not want to deal with either of them. She knew they were worried and eventually she would explain it all to them, just not right now, because right now all she could handle was work.

Livi spent most of that week hiding in her office. She discovered her eye cream did not reduce puffiness and redness as its label claimed, and she was not ready to answer any questions from anyone, especially not from Nadine. She avoided her assistant like the plague and was sickeningly grateful for the work Edward piled on her. She had lost her promotion, she had lost Jake, and all the extra work from Edward surprisingly helped her in her struggle to forget.

By Friday she was looking a little better even if she still felt horrible. Richard Harris, Nell's husband, had called her and asked her to meet him for lunch that day at DG's downtown. It was an odd place to eat lunch, but she knew the darkness would hide what remained of her eye problem.

"Livi! Over here!" said Richard, motioning her to a back booth when she walked in the pub's front door that afternoon. She felt as if she were returning to the scene of a crime when vague thoughts of Karaoke Tuesday came flooding back to her. Everywhere she went reminded her of Jake.

"Thanks for the invitation. I needed to get out of the office," Livi said as she sat across from Richard.

"No problem. Thanks for coming." Richard paused. "Uh, I'm sorry about Jake."

"Thanks. I'm sorry too," said Livi. She felt tears welling up in her eyes and was slightly embarrassed to lose it so easily in front of Richard.

Richard smiled at her. "It will be okay eventually," he said. He reached over and patted her hand.

Livi took a deep breath and said, "I know it will. Let's talk about something else." She wiped her eyes with a paper napkin.

"Well, I know you really have a lot on you right now, but I've run into something and you are the only one I can talk to about this," Richard said. He almost seemed nervous.

"What's up?" Livi asked.

"It's about Nadine," Richard said and stared hard at Livi. Before she could say anything, the waitress arrived to take their order. Fortunately, the menu was small and the order was quick so the waitress did not interrupt their now suddenly furtive meeting for long.

"What about Nadine?" Livi said as she took a sip of her water.

Richard cleared his throat and continued, "Okay. You know I mind my own business, and this is really not my deal, but things are so weird right now. I didn't know who to talk to, and then when I found out Nadine was involved I knew you had to know . . . "

"Richard," Livi interrupted. "You are rambling. One thing at a time. From the beginning. Now, what about Nadine?"

Richard took a deep breath and said, "Okay. Recently, I noticed a new cost account in our system. The account wasn't tied to any contract or vendor, and the money that Hampton Steel transferred into it was so minor that I really did not pay any attention to it. I just assumed it was for some special project, and I would be told about it eventually. You know how Hampton Steel works."

Livi nodded. Hampton Steel was notorious at being reactive and not proactive when it came to operations.

Richard continued, "Well, right about the time you closed the Turnkitt transaction, the money being transferred into the account increased—significantly. I mean, we are talking the account must have millions in it by now."

"Where is the money coming from?" Livi asked. None of this made sense to her. Hampton Steel had dozens of checks and balances to know exactly where every dime was spent.

"All over. A little here, a little there," Richard continued. "Someone has to be messing with the books for this to happen. It was a total accident that I ran into this account number. Just a fluke as I was making an entry into one of the other accounts. Hampton Steel's funds are being depleted into this one odd account and no one upstairs seems to know or care." Richard looked stressed and put his head in his hands. "At this rate, Hampton Steel will be bankrupt before we know it."

Livi's head was reeling and a lump entered her throat as she asked, "But what does this have to do with Nadine?"

Richard looked up and took another deep breath, "When I started seeing the amount of money being transferred, I wanted to know who was doing the transferring. I mean, someone else *had* to know what was going on. Well, I couldn't ask anyone in accounting. I assumed it was one of them. Who else had access to the books? So, do you know the really geeky computer guy that works in IT? Jim, with dark hair?"

Livi nodded.

"Well, he truly is a good guy," Richard continued. "Coaches the kids' soccer team with me. I trust him. Anyway, I asked him to see if he could figure out how the money was being transferred. I did not tell him everything I'm telling you. I just told him the information was needed by our auditors and that I would get in trouble if anyone knew I had asked for this. I made it sound like I had messed up and needed his help to cover things up with the auditors."

"Good thinking," Livi said. She was impressed by Richard's lying capacity with his IT guy.

"Well, he figured out where the transfers were coming from, all right." Richard leaned over the table and whispered, "Livi, all the transfers were initiated from Nadine's computer."

Livi sat back in shock. What had her assistant gotten herself into now? "But Nadine is not that smart! At least, I didn't think she was."

"Well, someone in your office is," Richard said as he leaned back into the booth again, letting Livi get a good grasp of what he was saying.

"You said the large transfers occurred right around the Turnkitt closing?" Livi asked. Her mind was processing Richard's revelations.

Richard nodded. The waitress brought their food but neither was hungry anymore.

"Which is right about the time Edward started. . ." Livi said, now thinking out loud.

"Yeah. . .?" Richard questioned.

"Richard, can you keep this to yourself for now?" Livi asked. "Consider the ball in my court. Give me some time to check out a few things." Livi wanted control of the situation.

"Sure," said Richard, seeming relieved that his burden had been passed on to Livi.

*

Jake sat at the lunch counter and absently pushed his fork around the hash brown casserole and honey baked ham sitting on his plate. Even though the special at The Diner today was Jake's favorite, he was not hungry.

Since returning to Millersville, Jake had become a regular at The Diner, and he used to look forward to his lunchtime break away from Nell's store. Lately, however, he was more somber, and even his favorite casserole today was not pulling him out of the slump he was experiencing.

Out of nowhere, chomping her gum and looking like a throw back from the 1950s, the waitress with the high bouffant placed a piece of cherry pie beside Jake's lunch plate.

Jake awoke from his trance and looked up. "What's this? I didn't order any pie," he said.

"I know. You just looked like you needed it. It's on the house," the waitress said as she continued to chomp her gum and move down the counter to pour coffee for her next customer.

Jake smiled a little, then continued to stare down at his casserole, losing his thoughts in the melted cheese and potato mush on his plate.

"Is this seat taken?" a familiar voice said behind him a few minutes later. Jake looked up to see Livi's father standing at the stool right beside him.

"No, sir," was all Jake said. Today's special just got a little uncomfortable.

"Mind if I sit?" Mr. Miller said.

"No, sir," said Jake, concentrating on his food again.

Mr. Miller took his seat and the two men simply stared down at the counter directly in front of them. The bouffanted waitress brought Mr. Miller a glass of ice water and took his order. Mr. Miller knew The Diner's menu well and today's special was one of his favorites. Jake overheard Mr. Miller's order and thought to himself that hash brown casserole could now be added to Livi and fly-fishing on the list of things the two men had in common.

"So, how have you been?" Mr. Miller broke the ice soon after the waitress left.

"I've been better," Jake said. He was nothing if not honest.

"So I've heard. Have you talked to her?" Mr. Miller asked.

"No. Have you?" Jake asked.

"Not really. Just heard you two aren't seeing each other." Mr. Miller paused. "I think I know why."

"I'm sure you know why. It's the same reason as last time," said Jake, finally looking up at Mr. Miller, their eyes meeting as if for the first time.

"I know and I'm sorry. My daughter has an easy way of messing up her personal life every time," Mr. Miller confessed. "But I love her—and I know you love her too. She means well. She just gets a little lost in her work sometimes."

"A little?" Jake said as he sarcastically raised his eyebrows at Mr. Miller.

"Okay, a lot. But maybe you could call her. Make the first move. If you all could just talk this thing out, I'm sure she would get it together this time." Mr. Miller said desperately. He spoke as if Jake were his last chance at straightening out Livi's priorities.

"If she wants to talk to me, she can call me," said Jake.

"You know she's not going to do that." Mr. Miller shook his head and sighed. "You two are both as stubborn as mules."

"Beats being a horse's ass," said Jake. He grinned and looked straight ahead as he took a sip of his water.

Mr. Miller smiled and looked over at Jake. He took one last shot at the situation with an openness that normally embarrassed a man from his generation. "Look, son, you two love each other. I know you do. But you are both set in your ways and, unless someone makes the first move, you both are going to lose out on the one thing that makes you two special. I was lucky enough to find the love of my life but lost her before our time was up. It'd be a real shame if you lost the love of your life before your life ever even gets started." Mr. Miller paused. "So do an old man a favor and call her, please."

"I'll think about it," said Jake as he took his last bite of hash brown casserole.

*

Livi sat in Hampton Steel's parking lot, car doors locked and engine still running. The sheriff's receptionist had placed her on hold and she nervously played with her purse strap waiting on Todd to answer.

"Hello," Todd finally said.

"Todd," Livi said. "It's Livi. Can you talk?"

"Sure. What's up?"

"I need a favor." Livi took a deep breath. "Do you remember when you offered to check out my new boss?"

"Yeah, but Livi, I was just joking," said Todd with a new tone.

"What if I'm not joking? I think Edward is embezzling from Hampton Steel and I need your help," Livi said. She knew she sounded desperate.

"Embezzling? That's a pretty strong accusation. What makes you say something like that?" asked Todd.

"One of Hampton Steel's accountants came to me with some funny money transfers and I believe Edward is behind it," Livi offered. She did not want to reveal Richard's involvement just yet.

"What evidence do you have?"

"Nothing specific yet. Just my gut instinct."

"You don't have anything specifically tying the transfers to Edward? Just your gut?" said Todd sarcastically.

"Yes. It sounds pretty bad when you say it like that. But seriously, Todd, can you help me?" asked Livi.

"No, not with just your 'gut instinct,'" Todd said matter-of-factly. He took his job as deputy seriously.

Livi was silent.

"Look," Todd finally said after Livi's prolonged silence made each of them a little uncomfortable. "You don't have any evidence for us to start a formal investigation. Go get some and then call me. But, in the meantime, what if I just make some calls myself? I don't mind doing a little undercover research on Mr. Winston. He did make my girlfriend's sister cry after all."

"Todd, thank you! I really appreciate this. If you have time right now, I can tell you what little I know about him. It's not much, but it is a place to start." Livi then relayed Edward's previous New York address and summarized her conversation with the realtor for Todd.

"Sounds like you are becoming quite the detective," Todd said, clearly impressed. "Look, if you think of anything else on him, just call me. I don't want to receive any emails at the department on this. Understood?"

"Oh, yeah. Good idea," Livi said. She felt like she was in the middle of a James Bond movie but it was Livi, not Sean Connery, who would be drinking the martinis in this one.

Livi hung up with her spirits slightly higher. She had taken action to resolve a problem and that always made her feel better. She left the security of her car and headed inside to her office. Nadine was not at her desk, as usual, and Livi was feeling particularly bold after her talk with Todd, so she sat down in front of Nadine's computer and started reading her assistant's email. She was hoping Nadine's email would prove her assistant had nothing to do with the money transfers.

Nervous nausea replaced Livi's butterflies as she scrolled through Nadine's inbox. Nadine could come back to her office any minute but Livi rationalized that she could just tell her assistant she was looking for a file. *Was Nadine stupid enough to believe that?*

The computer's inbox did not reveal anything so Livi moved on to Nadine's deleted emails. Immediately, Livi noticed there were a disproportionate number of deleted emails from Edward.

Livi started reading them and almost all of them were blank with just the word "Now" in the subject line. There were dozens like this, and Livi had no clue what they meant. Just when she was moving on to Nadine's sent file, Livi heard the familiar clicking of Nadine's heels coming down the hallway. Livi quickly closed Nadine's email, moved away from her assistant's desk and slid into her own office just as Nadine rounded the corner. Livi did not think Nadine saw her, but if she did, her assistant did not mention it.

Livi sat in her office the rest of the afternoon, scribbling the word "now" all over her legal pad. *What does that mean?* Livi thought. She did not believe her assistant could actually be involved with something as bad as embezzling. However, when the picture of Nadine and Edward talking at the party suddenly jumped to the front of Livi's mind, she realized Nadine could be involved with Edward for other reasons. She knew of Nadine's proclivity for sex, and Edward struck Livi as being sleazy enough to cheat on his wife. That combination convinced her that something was going on between them even if that something had nothing to do with Hampton Steel's money.

She was fortunate enough to avoid Nadine the rest of the day and was packing up to leave for the night when her cell phone rang.

"Hello," Livi said.

"Livi. It's Todd. I think I have something for you. Can you meet me at your dad's tonight? Elizabeth and I have plans to eat dinner with him, and I'd rather go over this with you somewhere away from your office or mine."

"Man, you are quick. Yeah, I can be at Dad's. Just set an extra plate for me." Livi said and hung up. She had not yet fully explained the Jake situation to her father or Elizabeth and dreaded the inevitable inquisition that would occur when she walked into her father's house that night. But her curiosity of Todd's findings overrode her dread, and she grabbed her briefcase and quickly headed out the door.

*

The house smelled like burgers, and Mr. Miller was obviously getting in one of his last grill sessions before fall officially closed in on him. Livi felt like she was getting ready to take her bar exam as she slowly walked down the home's hall to the kitchen. She assumed the inquisitors were waiting and she was right.

She found Elizabeth and Todd talking at the kitchen table with her father, who stood in the doorway leading to the back porch with spatula in hand. Voices hushed and eyes stared when she rounded the corner into the kitchen.

Of course, Elizabeth was the first to break the silence. She jumped out of her seat, bounded toward Livi and wrapped her arms tightly around her older sister.

"Oh, Livi. I've been so worried about you!" Elizabeth's concern was valid and Livi immediately realized how selfish she had been acting. Livi had been going through so much between her promotion and Jake but she had not thought at all how her life's recent changes affected her family.

Livi forgot her dread of the inquisition and instead felt guilty for causing her family to worry. While she was anxious to hear what Todd had to say, she knew she had to reassure her father and sister first.

"I know and I'm sorry," Livi said as she looked over at her father. "I'm fine, really I am. We all knew Jake and I were headed in different directions. Our crossroad just got here sooner than I thought it would."

"Look, Livi," Mr. Miller interrupted. "If you don't want to talk about it, that's fine with us."

"No, Dad, I'm good. Really. I have you all, don't I? Who needs a career or a guy when I have to deal with the two of you all the time?" joked Livi. She tried to be funny and Mr. Miller then knew she was on the road back to being herself. He just did not know that, in reality, Livi's newfound inner strength arose from her desire to crush Edward.

Mr. Miller put his arms around Livi. "Just remember God is in control," her father said, "and he never gives you more than you can handle."

"I know, Dad. Thanks," said Livi, hugging him back. "I'll be okay. Now let's eat. I'm starving." Livi was glad she had avoided the anticipated intense inquisition. She should have known her family would know just how to handle her at a time like this. They always had.

The quartet sat down at the table, leaving Mrs. Miller's chair empty as usual, and made small talk for the majority of the meal. Both Livi and Todd knew their conversation had to take place in private so, when the meal was finally finished, they headed to the living room while Elizabeth and Mr. Miller washed the dishes.

"So?" Livi asked. She was dying. It had taken everything she had to endure dinner without disclosing her true purpose for being there that night.

"Your gut may be right about Edward," Todd said in a hushed tone. "Now, before I tell you all this, you have to promise me you will keep this to yourself. Don't do anything. Let me handle it from here on out. Promise?"

"Whatever you say, Todd," Livi dismissively said amid her excitement.

"Livi, promise me," Todd spoke to her sternly. He knew her better than she thought.

"Okay! I promise! Geesh!" Livi said with a roll of her eyes.

"All right, here's the deal. I made a few calls and after talking to a friend of a friend of a friend—well, you get the picture—anyway, I finally got to a guy who works for the sheriff's department where Edward used to live. Apparently, they know him very well and were very pleased to find out he had settled here in Millersville."

"Really?" Livi asked. Her excitement was growing.

"Yeah, I found that fact interesting, too. Do you know anything about the company Edward worked for in New York—Newsome Industries?"

"No. I just know his father got him the job at Hampton Steel and that he sold his house very quickly to take Robert's place as general counsel," Livi replied.

Todd took a deep breath and continued, "Well, now his former company doesn't exist anymore. Apparently, Newsome Industries suffered some catastrophic financial loss which crippled it to the point of forcing the company to close. The rumor is that the loss was caused by some young accountant in the company's finance department embezzling a bunch of money."

"You're kidding?" Livi said. "That explains why Edward's father needed to find him a job so quickly. My new boss has expensive tastes. If he lost his job all of a sudden, he'd need to find something quickly to keep the money rolling in."

"I don't think that's the whole reason," whispered Todd.

"What do you mean?" asked Livi.

"That young accountant basically disappeared in the middle of this mess. Took the money and ran, so to speak, and no one has heard from her since. Not her parents, not her brother, not her friends. She just vanished along with the money."

"And?" Livi wanted Todd to get to the point.

"And at the time the accountant disappeared, the rumor mill implied she was having an affair with Edward," said Todd.

"Really?" Nadine's face immediately flashed in Livi's mind.

Todd continued, "Yeah. The local sheriff's department wanted to question him about the money and about the girl's disappearance but Edward left town before they could get to him. Now that they know where he is, they are sending a deputy down to talk to him. That's why I don't want you to say anything." Todd reminded Livi again. "Let us handle this. Okay?"

"Okay, okay. I got it," said Livi. "So it is not impossible that Edward is involved with the funny money transfers at Hampton Steel?"

"Not only is it not impossible, I think it is highly probable. According to the deputy I talked to, this guy is not on the up and up, and that is why I want you to stay away from him for now," Todd warned.

"Kind of hard with him being my boss and all," Livi replied.

"You're smart. I am sure you will think of something. Just lay low until after the deputy gets here and we talk to him. I'm serious, Livi. Can you do that?" he asked.

"Yes. Of course," said Livi, but despite all her false assurances to Todd, she was already planning her next move.

Chapter Sixteen

Livi drove as fast as she could to The Meadows. Todd's revelations made her think of one person and she wanted to get to him tonight. She had tried to leave her father's house quickly without anyone knowing how fast she wanted out of there. Luckily, her excuse of having too much work to do that night was one they had heard before.

As she drove through Millersville, her mind raced and, of course, Jake popped in her head. She wished she could talk to him about this. She missed him. Livi needed a confidante and, a few weeks ago, Jake would have been at the top of her list. But he was gone now, so she mentally moved on to the other man who had recently dominated her life, Robert Matthews.

Livi knew embezzlement was a serious charge, but she also knew she could confide in her legal mentor. The defeated look on her former boss's face the day she officially met Edward kept flashing in her mind. This new information about Edward would vindicate Robert to the board of directors and allow him to retire with dignity instead of as a beaten down junk yard dog.

If Edward and that accountant had embezzled from his former company, then the funny money transfers at Hampton Steel had to be related to Edward also. They just had to be. The two scenarios were just too similar. Livi just hoped Nadine was not really involved in this mess. Despite everything that happened recently, Livi still felt very protective of her high school friend.

Livi drove through The Meadows guard gate without any problem and made her way along the formally landscaped, winding roads to the home of Robert Matthews.

"Coming!" the voice from behind the door slurred. "Stop ringing that blasted bell! I'm moving as fast as I can!" the voice yelled.

The door opened without the front porch light ever being turned on. Livi could barely see into the home's darkness which was deeper than the outer night's shadows. When her eyes finally adjusted, she still could barely make out the figure stooping in the doorway.

"Robert?"

"Livi? What are you doing here?"

"Can I come in? We need to talk."

"Sure. Come on in!" Robert said as he stepped out of the doorway and fumbled for the lamp on the foyer table. With his back still toward Livi, he shuffled through the foyer's faint light into the home's library where his fingers struggled again, this time with the switch of an antique table lamp sitting on the corner of his desk.

His massive mahogany desk filled the center of the large room, which swelled with the old lawyer's life-long love of antiques. With the table lamp finally on, Robert literally fell into the large leather chair behind his mahogany desk, causing the chair to roll back abruptly and violently against the library's floor-to-ceiling bookshelves. He did not seem to notice the tough hit his antique books received from the desk chair and he thoughtlessly rolled himself back into place behind the desk as if nothing had happened. Finally, after much effort to put the desk chair back into its proper place, he looked up at Livi with half-closed eyes.

"Are you okay?" Livi asked. She knew the answer before the question came out of her mouth. She had seen him drunk before but never this drunk and alone.

"I'm fine, fine. What brings you out here this time of night?" Robert slurred. He looked small sitting slumped over in the large leather chair.

"I'm sorry. I didn't think it was that late," Livi said as she glanced at her watch. "Robert, it is just seven twenty-five."

"Oh. Must have lost track of time," he mumbled.

"Maybe I should come back another time," Livi said. She did not think Robert could help her tonight.

"No, no. You're fine. There may not be another time," he said. Robert's head bobbed back and forth as if he had lost all muscle control in his neck.

"What does that mean?" she asked.

"I mean there may not be another time. Damn, woman. Can't you hear?" he yelled.

Livi was shocked. Robert had never spoken to her like that. She had heard of angry drunks but never imagined her elegant Robert to embody one.

"Robert, I heard you," Livi said with a distinct calmness. "I just did not understand what you meant."

"Oh, forget it," Robert said as his head continued to bob. "What do you want?"

"I wanted to talk to you about Edward, but I can come back later if now is not a good time," said Livi.

"Edward!" Robert slurred as he perked up as much as a drunk in his state could perk up. "I'll tell you about Edward. He was forced on me just like this retirement thing. Never dreamed I'd go out like this! Put all that time into a company just to be shoved out like a dog. . ." Robert's words trailed off in a slur.

"You're drunk. We can talk later," Livi said as she turned to leave.

"Drunk! Of course I'm drunk!" Edward slurred defensively. "Wouldn't you be? Company crashing around me and all of a sudden I am the fall guy for Edward and whomever else wants to pile on the blame!"

"Blame?" Livi asked as her interest was piqued. "What are you talking about?"

"I'm talking about Hampton Steel! What do you think I'm talking about?" he responded.

Livi sat down in the chair across from Robert's desk and looked at him intently. Knowing she would regret getting Robert riled up in his current state, she reluctantly asked, "What do you mean 'fall guy'?"

"Fall guy. Stooge. You know. The guy everyone is going to blame when the company closes. Everyone is going to blame me for bringing Edward here and I did not do it!" the old lawyer bellowed.

When the company closes. Livi was floored. She never dreamed of Hampton Steel closing down. It was so vibrant, so vital to Millersville. Business had been great the past year and financials were flourishing, particularly with the Turnkitt deal closing. Shutting down Hampton Steel was the last thing anyone expected to happen.

Robert continued to ramble, at times incoherently, but Livi thought she could get more information if she allowed him to let off some steam. He was obviously due such a release and might say more tonight than he would when he was sober. Her goal to reveal Edward's true self to Robert had just changed from an exposé to a fact-finding mission.

"Is Hampton Steel closing?" Livi finally asked outright, interrupting Robert's muttering.

Robert sighed, "That's the plan according to Chamberlain. He brought in that Edward guy. Told me the young lawyer would handle things from here on out. Didn't find out Edward was brought here to close out the company until it was too late. The ball had already started rolling. I don't even think the rest of the board knows yet. Chamberlain's just pushing along without board approval. The slime ball tells me everyone will get severance but who believes him?" Robert's words were slurring and his head was bobbing more than before.

Livi was numb. She looked down at her fingers that nervously played with her coat button while she processed all this. If Hampton Steel closed, half of Millersville would be unemployed. The town could not sustain an unexpected blow like that. There would be nothing left of her hometown. And what did all this have to do with the money transfers from Nadine's computer? Was Edward reenacting his scheme from New York? *The whole town will be devastated.* Mr. Sullivan's words jostled around in Livi's head.

"What has Edward done to start closing the company down?" Livi asked as she looked up at Robert. At that moment, however, she realized her time for questioning had ended. Robert had passed out in his large chair, stomach protruding like a balloon, and drool literally dripping from his lips.

Livi was sad to see her mentor like this and was not sure whether she should leave him at his desk or try to move him to the library's large leather couch so he could lie down and fully sleep into soberness. She checked the distance between the desk and the couch and ultimately decided to leave Robert where he was. She was afraid such a move might rile his anger out of its deep sleep again. Livi quietly slid out the front door and into her car. *What now?* she thought as she headed home.

*

Livi could not sleep that night, or the next night, or the night after that. Knowing Edward was here to close down Hampton Steel was a secret burden she found hard to bear. She replayed the impact of the company closing over and over in her mind and could never escape the devastation that would fall over Millersville. Millersville's fragile economy was like an upside down pyramid with Hampton Steel housed in the bottom tip, supporting every other business in town.

If you didn't work for Hampton Steel, then someone in your family did. If your business didn't directly supply to Hampton Steel, then your business catered to clients who were employed by Hampton Steel. Hampton Steel was everywhere and its impending closure would swallow up Millersville like quicksand. Livi's hometown would disappear like so many other small towns in this economy and she imagined tumbleweeds rolling around downtown as if they were in the middle of an old Western movie.

She anxiously awaited Todd's call and her impatience combined with her imagination to convince her that the deputy from New York had questioned Edward, obviously found him guilty and was taking her new boss back to New York, thus foiling his evil plan to destroy Hampton Steel. However, in reality, Todd's call never came and it was apparent that the New York deputy was taking his own sweet time to get to Millersville. On top of that, Todd's response to her repeated phone calls to his office implied that he was quickly growing impatient with Livi's own eagerness. Livi, thus, spent her time working herself into a tizzy, unable to concentrate on anything else.

During the day, she shuffled legal papers around as she unsuccessfully tried to accomplish whatever mundane task Edward piled onto her. But late at night, in the comfort of her own home, she spent endless hours on the internet, trying to find out as much as she could about Newsome Industries and Edward's past life.

Information about the closing of Newsome Industries was plentiful as it apparently had impacted the small town in New York in the same manner Livi imagined Hampton Steel's closing would impact Millersville, Virginia. The local papers demonized the young accountant, Meg Smithson, and depicted her as a money-hungry young tart now assumedly in the Caribbean living off her loot from Newsome Industries.

The papers all said pretty much the same thing, but one article in particular stood out for Livi. Early on in the embezzlement investigation, one paper had published a human interest story on Ms. Smithson, detailing her life from an up and coming Harvard accounting graduate to a woman resorting to theft as a way to make it in this man's world.

While the sexist theme of the article was a little too cliché for Livi, the interview with Ms. Smithson's parents in Baltimore hit a soft spot. Even with all the evidence piled on Meg Smithson in the papers, her parents still strongly declared their daughter's innocence. Such loyalty reminded Livi of her own family and she faintly began to identify with the missing accountant.

Despite all this research and her now certifiable obsession of exposing Edward, Jake still occupied the nether corners of Livi's mind. Occasionally, he would show up right smack dab in the front of her memory bank when she was thinking about Millersville. However, since reminders of Jake were all over Livi's hometown, Livi was becoming quite adept at staying just busy enough with work to mentally push Jake back to where she thought he belonged, in her high school memory bucket.

It also helped that she had not really seen or talked to Jake since that fateful Saturday morning and her butterflies had long disappeared on a never-ending migration away from Livi's stomach. She thought about calling him a few times but decided against it. She even thought she saw him downtown one day but, instead of confronting him, she hid in the back seat of her car, not ready to face him or his green eyes.

She reasoned she could use her energy to win Jake back or keep Hampton Steel open, but she could not do both. After much deliberation, she chose Hampton Steel, assuming her role in Jake's life was long gone. He had not called her or made any attempt to contact her, so why waste her energy on a man who obviously did not want her or understand her? For the second time in her life, she had lost her life's other side and the butterflies that came with it.

In the end, she knew she was back to her one-sided life at Hampton Steel and this reluctant knowledge intensified her need to expose Edward and save her company and, thus, her job. Disregarding Todd's warning about lying low, Livi decided she needed to talk to the Smithsons face to face, to understand more about their daughter and her relationship with Edward. She also decided she needed a break from the Jake memories that continued to shout at her from every corner of Millersville. A trip out of town would literally and figuratively place some much-needed distance between Livi and her persistent Jake memories.

So one Friday night she impulsively packed an overnight bag and headed north up the interstate in her old BMW. It would be a four-hour drive to the Smithsons' home in Baltimore and, without Al Green singing in her car, she could easily find some quiet time to develop her plan and determine what to say to Meg's parents on the way up. Livi had not told anyone except her father that she was going away for the weekend and he had agreed to take care of Gatsby. She knew he assumed she was getting away as a result of the Jake situation, but she didn't correct him. If Mr. Miller knew his daughter was on an obsessive mission to expose her new boss's past in order to save Hampton Steel, he would most definitely not have let her go.

The drive up was uneventful with Livi's emotions alternating between anger for Edward and sadness for Jake. Livi eventually arrived in Baltimore and found a hotel near the Inner Harbor. Dropping her bags and collapsing onto the bed's down-filled comforter the minute she hit her room, she immediately fell asleep and her night became a restless mix of Jake dreams and Edward nightmares.

When her cell phone's ring woke her the next morning, it felt like time had stopped and she had only just entered her hotel room at that very moment. She was still clothed in yesterday's sweats as drool fell from her lips, and her agitated night had not given her any rest at all.

"Hello," she groggily slurped into the phone through her drool.

"Liv," the voice was soft and familiar. "It's Jake."

Livi instinctively sat up on the bed and looked at herself in the mirror hanging beside the television. The combination of Jake's voice and her strange hotel surroundings left her brain numb, but her always-present vanity was strong enough to push her into action at the sound of Jake's voice.

Smoothing down her bed-head hair in the mirror, she replied, "Hey Jake." But she stopped herself short when she realized she did not know what else to say. She had no speech planned, no rehearsed script for when she next spoke to him. So she just stopped talking as if she had nothing to say when in fact she had so much more swimming around in her tired head. She just did not know how to say it.

"Sorry to wake you. I. . .uh. . .I was wondering if I could stop by today to talk."

Jake sounded sad, or at least Livi wished he sounded sad.

"Um. . .I'm not home right now." She did not want to tell Jake about her impromptu wild-hair trip to Baltimore. He would have thought she was nuts.

"Oh. I didn't think. . .I mean. . .I hadn't thought of you not being. . ."

"No. No." Livi was shocked at Jake's assumption. "No, I'm not with anyone. I'm in Baltimore."

"Baltimore? Why?"

Here goes, thought Livi. "Uh. . .I'm here researching Edward, but don't tell anyone, okay?"

"Edward!" Jake boomed. "And here I was, thinking you were going through what I am but I was obviously wrong."

"But. . . but you don't understand," Livi protested.

"You're right. I don't understand." Jake hung up without saying or hearing another word.

Livi sat there for a long time, staring at her phone. The numbness previously restricted to her tired brain slowly moved throughout her entire body and Livi could actually feel it overtake her as she lay back on the hotel bed. She now knew what catatonic patients feel—nothing. No good, no bad, no pain, no joy—nothing. She even thought at one point that her heart stopped beating and she was almost glad for that. Almost glad for the death of her heart.

What a sad mess she had made of her life with nothing to show for it but a title on a business card. Jake was officially and irrevocably gone, her butterflies had abandoned her and now she was losing the only thing she had left—her company.

Livi did not know how long she lay there before her numbness eventually worked its way out of her system and left sadness in its wake. Inconsolable, cry till the comforter is soaked sadness. Livi's cry was so hard and lasted so long, she felt like she had run a marathon when it finally ended. Every memory she had pushed aside, every feeling she had repressed flooded out her tear ducts and landed on the down-filled comforter.

The past few weeks finally culminated in tear-induced dehydration as she sat alone in that strange hotel room in Baltimore and, when it was over, Livi thought her cry might not have been a bad thing considering the release she felt.

With her emotions running a gauntlet, anger soon replaced her sadness and she finally started to feel like herself again. Anger over Edward, anger over her job, anger over the resulting loss of Jake. There was nothing she could do about Jake now. He was gone forever. But she could do something about Edward and Hampton Steel. Her anger made her focus more intense and her resolve more robust and she eventually remembered why she was sitting alone in a Baltimore hotel in the first place.

Livi shook off her small pity party, quickly cleaned up, got dressed and, after a few strategically placed drops of concealer under her eyes, she implemented the plan she had concocted on her drive to Baltimore. After calling every "Tom", "Thomas" and "T. Smithson" in the phone book, she finally hit pay dirt with "T.W. Smithson".

"Hello," a lady answered.

"Mrs. Smithson?" Livi said, ready to embark on the conversation she had carefully staged in her mind.

"Yes?" said Mrs. Smithson.

"Mrs. Smithson, my name is Livi Miller and I'm calling about your daughter Meg. I was wondering if I could come by to ask you a few questions."

"You'll have to call back later and talk to my husband when he gets home. I don't talk to reporters anymore," Mrs. Smithson said and hastily hung up the phone.

Great, thought Livi. *She assumes I'm one of the bottom feeders.* She sat on the bed and stared out her hotel window over the Inner Harbor. She needed a Plan B. She had not thought of a Plan B on her drive up, only a Plan A, but now she obviously needed a Plan B.

She looked at the listing in the phone book again and noticed the Smithsons' zip code matched that of her hotel. The Smithsons had to live somewhat nearby. Determined to talk to someone in the Smithson family, she wrote down the address, grabbed her purse and headed to the hotel concierge. The concierge was extremely helpful and soon Livi was back in her car following the concierge's hand-written directions to the Smithson's home. She became lost and turned around twice but after two inquiring stops at the local Royal Farms gas stations she was headed back in the right direction.

After an unexpectedly short drive, she arrived at the Smithsons' home. It was a modest home located inside the Baltimore city limits in an area where two-story brick houses sat closely together with narrow yards and even narrower driveways. Most of the yards were surrounded by chain-link fences and the Smithsons' was no exception. Livi hesitantly parked in the driveway, blocking in a red, late model Ford pick up truck.

Just great. Ford people, Livi thought to herself. *Plan B is not starting off well.* She opened a small gate in the fence and made her way down the walkway toward the house. Closed curtains blocked Livi's view inside the home but she thought she saw someone peeking out of one of the second-story windows. Seeing the voyeur caused her to hasten her step and she quickly reached the front door.

Taking a deep breath to calm herself, Livi rang the doorbell. No one answered. She waited a few minutes and rang the bell again. After taking enough deep breaths to cause hyperventilation, Livi finally saw a shadow move behind the door's closed curtain. She heard the door's numerous locks being unlatched and the door swung open to reveal a large, strongly built, elderly gentleman standing in the doorway.

Behind him on the foyer wall, a large cross hung against old wallpaper imprinted with pink and yellow flowers and Livi was reminded of the faded antique wallpaper hanging in the Coopers' farmhouse foyer. The Jake memories would not even leave her alone here.

"Yes?" the man said. He was about her father's age but the lines on the man's face were deeper as if life's knife had cut him more than most people. His eyes were marine blue but tired and Livi could tell the man had no more fight left in him.

"Mr. Smithson?" she asked.

"Yes. Who are you?"

"Mr. Smithson, my name is Livi Miller and I would like to talk to you about your daughter Meg. I promise I am not a reporter. I am just doing a little research on Newsome Industries and Edward Winston and thought you might be able to help me."

The mention of Edward made Mr. Smithson's eyes mist red with anger. "Can't help you. Don't have anything more to say on the subject. Meg's gone and we don't know where she is. Don't know where Mr. Winston is either. Sorry," said Mr. Smithson as he started to close the door.

"Mr. Smithson, please," begged Livi as she stuck her foot out in the middle of the doorway, preventing the door from closing all the way. "Edward Winston is why I am here. He is working in Millersville, Virginia and I drove all the way from Millersville to talk to you about him. I know he is a bad guy and I need your help. I just want to know more about his relationship with Meg."

Mr. Smithson's eyes no longer revealed anger, but surprise. He opened the door slightly, "He is in Virginia?"

"Yes," said Livi.

"If he is in Virginia, then where is Meg?" Mr. Smithson said more to himself than to Livi.

"I don't know, but maybe we can figure this out together," Livi answered softly, realizing her visit had forced an unwanted revelation on Mr. Smithson.

"I. . .I need to go. I need to talk to my wife," Mr. Smithson's eyes saddened and he closed the door quietly but quickly in Livi's face.

Livi stood there staring at the door's closed curtain. She had gotten nowhere with this wild goose chase of a trip and now she had made matters worse by pouring the salt of Meg's disappearance alone and without Edward into the Smithsons' wounds. All this time, the Smithsons had assumed their Meg was with Edward, probably believing everyone's assumptions of a new Caribbean lifestyle, missing her but thinking she was living it up on a beach somewhere.

Now, the knowledge that Edward was in Virginia would force them to confront Meg's fate as being very alone and they would have to search even harder within themselves for the reason they had not heard from Meg. Saddened by these thoughts, Livi stuck her business card with her cell phone number in the crack of the door in case Mr. Smithson changed his mind, and then made her way slowly down the walkway to her car.

She pulled out of the driveway and headed back toward her hotel, frustrated by her inability to accomplish anything of late and disappointed with herself for being unable to foresee how her recent actions impacted others.

She drove about a block from the Smithsons' house before stopping at a red light. There were very few cars at the intersection and she took the brief timeout granted by the stoplight to start thinking about where she should go next. Suddenly, out of nowhere, a boy's face appeared at Livi's driver-side window and scared the contemplative young attorney half to death. The boy beat on Livi's window and held up her business card. He looked to be about seventeen and wore an oversized, black U2 tee shirt that made his skinny little arms appear even skinnier. He was breathing heavily as if he had just run the sprint of his life.

"Pull over!" the boy shouted as he pointed to the shoulder of the road.

"What the . . . ?" Livi just stared at the blonde-haired boy while still waiting for the light to turn green.

"Please!" the boy yelled through the car's thick window glass as he shoved Livi's business card against her window again, "I'm Mike Smithson! Meg's brother!"

Livi quickly pulled her car over just as the light turned green. She was not sure what was happening but the look on the boy's face prompted her to do what he asked. Mike Smithson quickly slid into Livi's passenger seat and shut the door. He looked her up and down as if he himself was now not sure what to do next.

"Hi," the boy finally said.

"Hi," said Livi, still not understanding why Meg's younger brother was sitting in her front seat.

"I heard you talking to my dad. Uh, sorry he was so short with you," young Mike Smithson was now growing hesitant.

"That's okay. Your family has been through a lot. I'm sorry if I said anything to upset him."

"No, everything's cool. It will take some time for them to process, but in the end, it will be better for them to know."

"To know what?" asked Livi.

"To know Meg's dead," said Mike Smithson very matter-of-factly.

"I never said. . ." Livi was very confused.

"You didn't have to." The boy sighed and stared into Livi's eyes as if he were searching for something. Finally, he continued, "Look, everyone assumes that Meg took all that money and she is living on a beach somewhere. My parents always thought that Mr.

Winston was with her, that she fell in love with him and they ran off together. A little too romantic for me, but thinking that made it easier for my parents to come to grips that Meg was gone."

"And me telling them Edward was in Virginia just ruined that for them." Livi's assumption about herself was right. Her impulsiveness hurt the Smithsons.

"It's fine really. My parents will be okay eventually. I made peace with her death a long time ago."

"You sound so sure. Why do you automatically assume she is dead?" Livi did not think Mike's steps were logical.

"Look, our family is close. Meg talked to Mom every day and she would not just take off without talking to one of us or letting us know she was okay. She was not that kind of girl. She never liked her family to worry about her. It's been so long since Meg talked to anyone in her family, my parents convinced themselves that she was too busy with Mr. Winston to contact us and that she would eventually come to her senses and come home."

"But you think she is dead?" Livi asked as she tried to follow the boy's rationale. "You never believed she was with Edward? Why not?"

"Because my sister would not be caught dead with Mr. Winston or any other man. My sister was gay. There is no way she would have left town with some guy, no matter how much money was involved."

Livi was stunned. All her assumptions about Meg just flew out the window. "Your sister was a lesbian? So she wasn't having an affair with Edward like everyone said?"

"No way! Look, not many people knew she was gay—just me and a few of her close friends. As far as my parents and everyone else were concerned, I thought it was better for them to think she was living it up on some beach with a guy instead of knowing she was gay."

"Why," asked Livi. None of this made sense to her.

"Ms. Miller, my family is Catholic. It is way better for my

family to think of my sister as someone who embezzles for her boyfriend rather than someone who's a lesbian. You might not understand, but I could not hurt my parents any more than they already were. If they knew she was gay, it would kill them."

"I understand. Really, I do," said Livi. Being Baptist, Livi understood all too well a religion's impact on a family's dynamics.

"So, if she isn't with Mr. Winston and she isn't on a beach somewhere with all that money, I think she's dead. I don't know how—I just know in my heart she is dead. Otherwise, she would have contacted us."

"I'm sorry." Livi did not know what else to say.

"Me too."

"Why did everyone think Meg was having an affair with Edward?"

"I don't know. Maybe because they worked a lot of deals together. Maybe because they both disappeared at the same time. Who knows? People love to gossip and at Newsome Industries everything was a soap opera—at least that is what my sister said."

"Did you ever tell the police any of this?"

"No. Like I said, my sister being a lesbian would have killed my parents. Besides, Meg told me that Mr. Winston was one sleazy dude. I did not want to go anywhere near that guy. My parents already lost one kid. I didn't want to be next." Mike's overly dramatic implications about Edward scared Livi.

"You don't think. . .?" Livi was actually speechless.

"I don't know. I know he scared Meg. She told me so. I just never knew how much he scared her but then she disappeared, and, well, you know the rest," Mike said as he stared out the car's front window. He leaned up and reached in the back pocket of his jeans to pull out a small book. "I don't know if this will help, but here's Meg's diary. If you're dealing with that Mr. Winston guy, you're gonna need all the ammo you can get. My parents don't know anything about Meg's diary but I'd really appreciate you giving it back to me after you're finished with it. Now that she is gone, that pretty much all I have left of her."

"I promise to give it back to you as soon as I can," Livi could not believe Mike was trusting her with so much. "Why are you letting me see this?"

Mike looked up at Livi intently and said, "Your eyes. They remind me of my sister's. Besides, if this helps you with Mr. Winston, then maybe it's kind of like I'm helping Meg in a way. Understand?"

"I think so. Thank you," Livi said as she gently took the book from the boy's hands. "I promise to take really good care of this."

"I know you will. Just send it back to me when you're done—and please don't let anyone else see this. Like I said—I really don't want my parents hurt any more than they already are."

"You have my word," said Livi.

"Thank you," Mike said as he leaned over and gave Livi an unexpected hug. He exited the car without saying another word, running out of Livi's life as quickly as he ran in.

Livi drove back to her hotel as fast as she could and spent the night reading Meg's diary. It was more a journal than a diary with a worn outer jacket covered with faded flowers and Meg's pen doodles. The young accountant had not written in the journal every day but instead had used the empty pages to vent the feelings and frustrations life had piled on her—being a woman working in a man's world, being a closeted lesbian, living up to the reputation that preceded any graduate from Harvard.

Meg had taken all these stresses and released them onto the pages of her journal as if regurgitating these problems into this book made them escape her and find their home among the pages.

Livi thought the entire book was a little depressing and not at all helpful until she came upon an entry Meg wrote about three months before she disappeared. It was the first time Meg's journal mentioned Edward and it was obvious Meg hated Edward as much, if not more, than Livi did. Somehow, Meg did not know how, but somehow, Edward had discovered her sexual orientation secret. As Livi continued to read, it was obvious that Meg feared exposure by Edward and any resulting impact on her career and family. Livi could not imagine how difficult Meg's life at Newsome Industries became with Edward holding her secret over her head, using her position for his own financial gain.

Edward apparently blackmailed Meg with his knowledge that she was gay, and forced the young accountant to discretely move Newsome Industries funds around from account to account. The distress in Meg's entries was enough to make Livi cry as she thought of the young girl carrying this burden alone, torn between hurting her family and compromising her own principles.

The journal revealed that Meg's embezzling for Edward continued the entire three-month time span prior to her disappearance. Finally, Meg apparently reached her breaking point and it was obvious she had decided to stop working for Edward. This particular journal entry revealed a determination that Livi had not seen in the book's previous pages and it almost made Livi proud to discover that Meg was going to stand up to Edward, to fight against the power he held over her.

As Livi turned the page, her heart suddenly fell as she realized Meg's determined entry, the entry that was going to change the young accountant's life, was ultimately her final entry. The remaining pages of the journal were blank. She would never know the outcome of Meg's fight. Livi only knew it was her last.

*

Livi's drive back to Millersville was a blur of silence. No sound came from the radio and Livi had only her thoughts to keep her company. She drove along the interstate and continuously replayed the past few weeks in her mind. It seemed like forever since she had lunch with Richard and started on this confusing journey. She now had all this information, but she had no idea what to do with it.

Every now and then, Jake popped into the middle of her thoughts, but she would quickly push him back in her memory stockpile as she instead contemplated her next move. She needed to do something, to take action, to stop Hampton Steel from closing.

She needed to talk to someone about this, but she did not know who would believe her. She was not especially close to the CEO or other upper management. Most of her work had been through Robert and a select few board members. A few miles outside Millersville, a light bulb finally turned on in Livi's head. That was it. She needed a board member. She needed Joseph Sullivan. He would know what to do.

"Hello?" the old man answered on the second ring.

"Mr. Sullivan? It's Livi Miller," she said, trying not to sound nervous. "I know it is getting late but I really need to talk to you about something."

"Well, sure, Livi. What do you need?" asked Mr. Sullivan.

"Uh, I would prefer to speak with you in person. It. . .it's about Edward Winston. I need the advice of a board member. Do you mind? I am actually near The Meadows and can be there in about five minutes," Livi lied, her nervousness slowly leaving her.

"Sure. No problem. Come on by," said Mr. Sullivan. "I'll see you then."

Livi felt slightly better as she redirected her driving route to the Sullivan house. She pulled into the expansive concrete driveway exactly four minutes later and started walking to the front door. The last time she walked this way she had been holding Jake's hand. This thought made Livi's heart a little heavier, so she pushed yet another Jake memory to the back of her mind. She needed to concentrate on Edward and Hampton Steel and did not need Jake constantly popping into her head tonight.

Unlike Robert's house a few days ago, Mr. Sullivan's home glowed tonight with light and the bright front porch was welcoming as Livi rang the doorbell. Mr. Sullivan opened the door with a smile and motioned her inside.

"I'm so sorry to catch you this time of night," said Livi as she entered the home's foyer.

"No problem, dear. Come on in the study," said Mr. Sullivan as he led her through the living room. "I hope you don't mind but we had another board member here for dinner tonight, so I asked him to join us. You said you needed a board member's advice, so I figured two of our heads are better than one. I hope we can help you."

Livi rounded the corner into the study and there sat the one board member she did not want or need to see tonight—Alexander Chamberlain, the man who brought Edward to Hampton Steel. This was not good.

"Hello, Olivia." Mr. Chamberlain smiled and asked, "How can we help you tonight?"

Chapter Seventeen

Damn, Livi thought. She stood frozen in the middle of the room. Todd had told her to leave it alone. She now wished she had listened to him.

"You know, this can wait. You all obviously had dinner plans and I don't want to interrupt," said Livi as she tried to think of a gracious way out of there.

"No, you're fine, dear," Mr. Sullivan said as he sat down across from Mr. Chamberlain. "We finished dinner and are just shooting the bull. Now, tell us. You said something about Edward?"

Livi looked at Mr. Chamberlain who smiled at her. His smile reminded her of someone but she could not place it at that moment. She tried to think of another excuse to get out of there, but then it hit her. What did she have to lose? Hampton Steel's predetermined fate ensured she would definitely lose her job if she did not say anything.

If she did tell the two board members what she knew, she at least had a fifty/fifty shot at either being fired or possibly stopping the company's closing. Quickly analyzing her situation, she decided to spill the beans.

"Well, I hope I am not speaking out of turn," Livi directed her statement to Mr. Sullivan, "but I found out some things that I thought you should know. I've already spoken to Robert, and, after some additional research, I decided the matter's urgency required me to meet with you tonight, Mr. Sullivan."

"I'm sure we can address whatever your concerns are, Olivia," Mr. Chamberlain replied.

"I sincerely hope so. First, I. . .I know about Hampton Steel closing. Robert told me," Livi said matter-of-factly and again directed her statements to Mr. Sullivan.

"I'm sorry you found out that way, Olivia," replied Mr. Chamberlain. "I always knew that drunk would tell someone. Please be assured that we intend to adequately compensate all the employees for their job losses. Of course, the higher you are on the ladder, the more you will receive so you should be expecting a nice, tidy sum for yourself."

Mr. Sullivan just sat there in silence, obviously having lost total control of the conversation that he was not a part of to begin with.

Livi turned pointedly to Mr. Chamberlain, "I also know you brought Edward in to finish off the company's closing. Robert is afraid he will get blamed for Edward's involvement, but I am sure you will set the record straight on who hired Edward, won't you?" Livi asked. "I mean you are his father's friend, right?"

"Father's friend?" Mr. Chamberlain said and smiled. "Yes, I know his father very well. Of course, I will take credit for hiring Edward. I'm sure people will love him once they see the amount of their severance checks."

"Did you know anything about Edward before you hired him?" Livi asked Mr. Chamberlain.

"I knew enough," said Mr. Chamberlain.

"Did you know he was suspected of embezzling at his old company?" Livi asked. She was not holding anything back. She had nothing to lose.

"Who told you that? That is ridiculous," scoffed Mr. Chamberlain, glancing at Mr. Sullivan with a newly acquired nervousness.

Mr. Sullivan's face changed from passive to inquisitive as he sat up straighter in his chair. "Livi, what are you talking about?" he queried.

Livi took a deep breath and said, "Apparently, Edward's former company, Newsome Industries, suffered some sort of crippling financial loss directly attributed to some young accountant embezzling. Mr. Winston was apparently blackmailing this accountant, forcing her to embezzle significant amounts of money from Newsome

Industries. The girl and the money disappeared and before the police could question Edward about it, he disappeared as well." Livi paused. "At least, they thought he disappeared. They now know he is in Millersville and are on their way to talk to him this weekend."

Mr. Chamberlain stared at Livi hard. She had obviously, but unknowingly, touched a nerve in the old man's armor.

Mr. Sullivan looked shocked and gasped, "Livi, how do you know all this?"

"The police," was all Livi said. It was the truth, just not the whole truth. She did not want to get into Richard's and Todd's involvement or her recent trip to Baltimore right now.

"I'm sure there is a valid explanation for all this," Mr. Chamberlain said in an attempt to assure Mr. Sullivan.

"I hope there is also an explanation for the strange money transfers out of Hampton Steel as well," Livi continued. "Apparently, since the Turnkitt closing, large sums of money have been transferred out of Hampton Steel and into some strange account not related to any project at the company. I believe if Edward embezzled once, he can do it again."

"Livi," Mr. Chamberlain began, regaining his control of the conversation. "We appreciate your concern for the company and I promise you we will look into these money transfers you mention. Obviously, however, knowing what you think you do about Edward, it will be hard for you to work for him going forward."

"If the company is closing, there is no 'going forward,'" said Livi with a smirk.

"Exactly!" Mr. Chamberlain continued. "So maybe it would be best if you let the board handle Edward and these alleged money transfers. You can go ahead and take your severance now and get out of this mess entirely. Travel. Take a trip somewhere warm. I'm sure there is a lot you can do with three times your salary," Mr. Chamberlain said with a smile.

"Wait. . .are you. . .are you firing me?" Livi said. She looked over to Mr. Sullivan who just sat there, shocked into silence.

"No. You aren't being fired," Mr. Chamberlain tried to explain. "Just think of it as getting a head start on your severance with the company closing. Everyone will be in your shoes in a few weeks. You are just getting a jump on them and the Millersville job market.

"You are a smart girl. Take the money and run, so to speak. It's still an early night, why don't you head back to your office and think about it. Shoot! You could even pack up tonight and be on the beach tomorrow. We'll just wire your severance payment directly to your bank account. How does that sound?" Mr. Chamberlain made it all sound so easy.

Livi had suspected she could lose her job by exposing Edward, but deep down she did not really think it would happen. She looked at Mr. Sullivan who by now had turned pale and looked like he had seen a ghost. He obviously had no clue about Edward's past or the funny money transfers out of Hampton Steel. He was truly in a state of shock, and Livi doubted her perfunctory job loss was registering in the old man's brain.

She needed to get out of there and get somewhere she could think. Mr. Chamberlain was right about one thing. Her office was quiet this time of night, and she could pack up her things and be out of there before morning.

That way she would not have to face anyone as a recently fired Hampton Steele employee. She could pack up her office tonight and avoid seeing all the stares from her coworkers who would soon be losing their jobs as well. Livi looked hard at Mr. Chamberlain, turned around, and walked quickly out of the house and to her car without saying another word. She needed a new action plan.

*

"I don't care where you are. Get to the office now! I think she's on her way there to pack up," the other man said. "You need to take care of things tonight. The police are on their way to question you about New York, so we need to complete the transfers and finish this thing now!"

"Chill out, Daddy Dearest, I have it under control," said Edward, holding his cell phone and turning the steering wheel at the same time. "I'm turning around right now. I can be at the office in ten minutes."

"Can you close out the account tonight?" Alexander Chamberlain sounded worried. His son did not always do as he was told.

"Sure," Edward said, pleased with himself. "I've already got that covered. Just get the plane ready. I want to be on that bird tonight."

"It will be ready. You don't need to worry about that," his father said. "By the way, what did you tell your wife?"

"Nothing. She'll be fine as soon as I send her some money and sign the divorce papers. I really think she'll be glad to see me go." Edward paused. "Oh, that reminds me. Tell the pilots there will be three passengers now, not two."

"Who else is going with us?" Chamberlain asked. He did not like his son making plans without him.

"My lucky charm," said Edward.

*

Edward parked around the corner from Hampton Steel's corporate offices and made his way up the front walk and into the large glass building without being seen. It would be foolish to park in his executive space tonight, so he was pleased to find a parking place on an empty side street so close to Hampton Steel's offices.

He made his way through the cold, cavernous lobby and headed straight to the legal department. This late at night there was not a soul in the building as he walked through Nadine's office and entered Livi's. She was not there yet, so he stood there in the dark office trying to figure out the best place for him to accomplish his chosen task tonight. He knew what he had to do. Luckily, he had done it before.

Because it was not his first time, it felt easier than he remembered and, after perusing her office, he soon spotted a statue on the bookcase behind her desk. He picked it up and felt its weight. "The Business Journal's Young Lawyer Award—Olivia Grace Miller" was inscribed on the base of the Lady Justice statue.

Good thing this lady's wearing a blindfold tonight, Edward thought as he fingered the face of the statue. The rough edges of the statue's form might leave too many jagged edges, which could result in more blood than he liked but the weight felt right and he did not see anything else in the office that would satisfy his need tonight. Edward then slid behind Livi's office door. He left the door only slightly cracked, allowing a sliver of light from Nadine's office to fall onto Livi's beige carpeted floor.

As he stood there, staring at the sliver, he heard her coming. Time seemed to stop while he counted her steps toward him. His breathing fell into rhythm with his counting and became his calm before his storm. Each inhale and exhale acted like a metronome for his movements as he calculatingly raised the statue high.

With one final thrusting exhale, he smashed the statue down with a deep, forceful thud on the woman's head just as she entered the dark office. Her limp, lithe body fell hard against the office door, pushing it wide open. The sliver of light expanded and descended like a shroud over her body to reveal the mistaken target of Edward's anger.

"What have I done?" breathed Edward as the woman's scarlet blood spread through the light falling on the now not-so-beige carpet.

Chapter Eighteen

The phone rang four times, waking Livi up.

"Hello?" Livi groggily answered. She had been in a deep sleep and obviously was not expecting a call from Hampton Steel or anyone else at two o'clock in the morning.

"Ms. Miller?"

"Yes. Who is this?" Livi asked, still trying to wake up.

"It's Sherman, the night guard at Hampton Steel. I'm sorry to wake you but you need to get down here as soon as possible. I've already called the police, but I think you need to be here too," he said.

"The police? What's going on?" Livi asked. She was waking up now.

"Uh, I think it's best if you just come on down here, Ms. Miller. Please come as quick as you can," said Sherman and he hung up.

Livi got dressed as fast as she could. She could not imagine anything going on at Hampton Steel that required her presence at two in the morning. Earlier, she had decided not to go to the office that night after all but was so keyed up from her meeting with Mr. Sullivan and Mr. Chamberlain that she had taken a mild sedative to help her get to sleep. Livi's inexperience with sedatives combined with the very early hour of that morning to make her more than a little groggy as she drove to Hampton Steel.

But soon, before she even reached the company's parking lot, her mind instantly overcame the sedative's lingering aftereffects when she saw the multitude of emergency lights surrounding Hampton Steel. With her heart racing, Livi parked as close as she could, but an ambulance and five sheriff's cars blocked the building's front walkway so she had to wind her walk through the many emergency vehicles just to get to the front door. Sherman met her in the lobby, his hands fidgety.

"Ms. Miller, I am so very sorry," the guard said with tears in his eyes.

"Sherman, I am sure everything will be fine. Now what is going on?" Livi asked. She was concerned now.

"Please follow me," said the guard as he led Livi toward the legal department. They got to her suite of offices, and Livi spotted Todd standing near Nadine's desk. The deputy looked up and immediately walked over to her. He was obviously upset but was keeping it under control while in deputy mode. Sherman silently passed Livi over to Todd and left the office.

"Todd, what in the world is going on?" Livi asked, scared. She had never seen Todd upset like this.

"Livi, I've got some bad news," said Todd putting his hands on her shoulders. Livi could see people milling about her office, and she strained to see what was going on beyond Todd's arms.

"What is it?" said Livi as she forcefully broke free from Todd's grasp. She ran to her office, pushing aside the milling deputies. There on the floor lay Nadine, her lifeless body surrounded by her own blood. "No! No!" screamed Livi just as Todd caught her at the doorway. She turned away from Nadine and buried her head in Todd's chest.

"Livi, I'm so sorry. I didn't want you to see her like this," said Todd as he held her close. He escorted Livi back to Nadine's office where she sat in Nadine's chair and cried uncontrollably, unable to catch her breath. She felt dizzy and nauseous and was not fully aware of what was happening around her. The room was spinning as Todd tried to calm her down and Livi felt like she could not wake up from this bad dream.

People were talking to her but it was as if they were speaking a foreign language. She could not understand what they were saying nor could she speak herself. Everything was in slow motion, and she was on the verge of both throwing up and passing out when he appeared at the door.

In the middle of her craziness, there stood Jake. In one long stride, he walked from the doorway to Livi and wrapped his large, muscular arms around her without saying a word. He shielded her from the detectives, their questions, and the dizzying room, and once again his shoulder became her pillow. She cried and cried in his arms until there was nothing left. After what felt like a very long time, she finally composed herself and looked up at him with questioning eyes.

"Todd called me," Jake said, answering her silent question.

"I hope you don't mind," said Todd from behind her.

"No. Thank you, Todd," said Livi as she slightly smiled at Jake. "And thank you for coming, Jake."

"No problem," said Jake as he held her close.

While still in Jake's arms, Livi looked over to her deputy friend and asked, "Todd, what. . .what happened?" Livi was still in shock.

"We don't know," Todd answered. "Sherman was making rounds and found her lying there. She was hit in the head with one of your awards."

"But who would do something like this?" Livi asked.

"We don't know. Maybe if you could answer some questions from the detectives, we might get a head start on the investigation," said Todd, looking at her strangely.

"You don't think this had anything to do with the money transfers, do you?" Livi asked. She now understood Todd's strange look.

He sighed. "Maybe. Just tell the detectives all you know. Then they will take it from there. Okay?"

"Sure," said Livi.

"Do you want me to stay with you while you talk to the detectives?" asked Jake without any reservation.

"Please, if. . .if you don't mind," said Livi gratefully.

The two detectives sat down on Nadine's desk and faced Livi, still seated in her assistant's chair. Jake stood by her side and did not move as Livi told the detectives everything, from the wire transfers, to Hampton Steel's closing, to her suspicion of Edward's affair with Nadine, to Edward's blackmail and Meg's resulting disappearance. She held nothing back. She only got choked up once more as she saw the coroner wheel Nadine out of the office in a body bag.

Jake looked down at her and squeezed her hand, and she was soon back on track with her story for the detectives. By the time she finished, the entire Millersville sheriff's department was looking for their prime suspect, Edward.

"Can I go now?" Livi asked Todd when the questioning concluded.

"Sure. But Jake has to drive you home. I don't want you on the roads after being this upset. Departmental policy. Understood?" Todd asked both Livi and Jake.

"No problem," said Jake. Livi nodded in agreement. The two made their way through the many deputies and emergency vehicles toward Jake's truck in the Hampton Steel parking lot.

"Are you sure you don't mind taking me home?" asked Livi when they reached the truck.

"Of course not," said Jake as he opened her door. When they were both inside the truck, Jake looked over at her tenderly and held her hand.

At the touch of Jake's skin, she faintly felt her butterflies arrive home, slowly, just a few at a time, but definitely a homecoming from their long, unwanted migration. "I'm glad Todd called you," said Livi.

"Me too," said Jake as he stared into her eyes and smiled. He reluctantly let go of her hand and started the engine. Their ride was silent as each processed the events of the night and how these events affected their relationship. Neither knew how to resolve their differing opinions on Livi's career but, at that moment, they were together and that fact alone was soothing to them both. They arrived at Livi's house, each without answers but both feeling more positive than they had in a while.

"Are you okay?" Jake asked as he walked Livi to her front door.

"I don't know. I am so tired I can't even think straight." Livi stared hard into Jake's green eyes.

"Why don't you get a good night's sleep and call me tomorrow," said Jake, knowing just what Livi needed in his caretaker mode.

"Sure. Thanks for everything. I. . .I mean it," said Livi, her own blue eyes intense as her butterflies got comfortable again.

Jake leaned down and kissed her forehead, his hand resting on her cheek like a crutch. "Sleep tight and I'll see you tomorrow," he whispered as he turned to head back to his truck.

Livi opened her front door, lost in the confusing events of the night. On the one hand, she mourned the loss of her friend but, on the other hand, seeing Jake gave her a little hope. In the midst of these contrasting feelings, she felt that something was not quite right as she turned to close the door behind her and she realized Gatsby had not met her at the door as he normally did.

She looked down the long hallway into her kitchen and saw the back door cracked open. As she headed down the hallway to investigate, she saw something move in the living room out of the corner of her eye and, as she realized what she was looking at, stomach nerves forcibly pushed away her butterflies. There, sitting in her living room with a fire blazing in the fireplace, was the one entity who symbolized pure evil in her world.

"Hello, Olivia," said Edward.

Chapter Nineteen

Jake slowly walked back to his truck, meditating on the past few hours. He had no regrets about taking Todd's call and was glad he could be there for Livi. Despite everything that had been said between them and Livi's love for her work, Jake still needed her, still loved her.

He was torn between running back to her and begging to hold her through the night, to make every bad thing from tonight go away on the one hand, and, on the other hand, to swallow his pride and accept the realization that Livi's work ethic would never change.

His truck was parked on the street in front of Livi's house and the cool fall air flowing through the lowered windows erased the tiredness he felt earlier. He sat there, not wanting to leave but not needing to stay. He fumbled with his keys as if somehow they would decide his internal debate. After what seemed like an eternity, he finally decided that practicality dictated he wait until morning to talk to Livi so he inserted his keys in the ignition.

Suddenly, a terrified, high-pitched scream pierced the silence of Jake's night.

"Livi!" he yelled.

*

The fire roared in the seldom-used living room fireplace and the room glowed like hell with the devil, Edward, sitting in the middle of it.

"Where's my dog? How did you get in here?" Livi asked. She was visibly shaking and again on the verge of throwing up. Her thought processes stopped working and she just stood in the hallway, unable to move.

"Puppy is fine. He's probably off somewhere napping. That will happen when you down a bottle of your master's sleeping pills. That dog really likes that nasty canned dog food you feed him. Lucky for me he was hungry." Edward smirked then sternly said, "Sit down, Olivia. We need to have a little talk."

Livi did not move. Edward's eyes were glowing in the firelight and she knew she was dealing with a crazed man.

"I said sit down!" Edward yelled as he picked up the fireplace poker and lunged at her.

Livi moved into the living room and quickly sat down on the couch, never taking her eyes off Edward.

"Why didn't you go to your office tonight like my father told you to?" Edward asked. He paced the living room floor, swinging the poker from side to side like a pendulum. The fire roared behind him and cast a weird glow around Edward's form.

"Your father?" Livi asked. The mention of her office tonight confirmed Livi's suspicions. She was in the presence of a heartless killer.

"My father. Alexander Chamberlain. Your Chairman of the Board. You hadn't figured that one out yet?" Edward said and sarcastically smiled. "Maybe you are not as smart as everyone says."

Livi tried to process what was happening to her. Alexander Chamberlain's smile flashed in her mind, and she now realized the resemblance between father and son.

"Yes, dear old Dad. So proud that he could rescue his illegitimate son from his New York predicament. But you know all about that, don't you?" Edward continued.

Livi sat, silently wishing she had asked Jake to stay.

"Yeah. I hear you have deputies coming to town just to talk to me. I feel so very, very special!" Edward said and laughed with an insane cackle. "You think you are so smart. Finding out about my little scheme in New York. My little accountant friend was helpful but she just couldn't get enough out of that dying company to set me and Daddy Dearest up for life," Edward said.

He paused and looked at the ceiling with an odd look on his face. "She was useful until she had to die. Felt bad about that. Really, I did. But, you see, we needed everything about New York to just disappear. You can understand that, can't you?" Edward was rambling, almost talking to himself instead of Livi. He paced, wild eyes roving as he swung the poker back and forth, back and forth.

Livi glanced over to the front door.

"Don't even think about it!" Edward yelled. He jumped to her, pulled her off the couch, and pushed her to the floor with strength forged by adrenaline. He pinned her arms down with the poker, his face so close she could smell his alcohol-tinged breath. "You can't leave. You owe me for my sweet Nadine!" he growled.

All Livi could see were Edward's crazed eyes glowing in the firelight. He sat on top of her and used the poker to shackle her so she was not able to move one muscle. She was trapped on her own living room floor beneath this mad man and she saw no way out.

"Sweet, sweet Nadine," Edward was saying as his fingers traced the outline of Livi's face. "She truly was my soul mate. She got me, you know? She understood why I do the things I do. She was different from everyone else. Nadine was my equal in every way. Sure, she didn't come up with the plan to transfer money out of Hampton Steel. But she actually put my plan in motion and, best of all, she did it out of love. She loved me and now she's gone and it is all your fault!"

Edward slammed his fist on the floor beside Livi's head. "You were supposed to be in that office tonight, not her! Not her! And for that, you need to pay, Miss Olivia, you need to pay!" he roared.

Edward stared down at Livi and she could practically see the evil wheels turning in his calculating mind. He held the poker tightly across Livi's chest with one hand and started reaching for her pants with the other. "I know. If I can't have Nadine, you'll just have to do," he said in a voice suddenly calmer.

Realizing Edward's next move, Livi screamed. She screamed with all she had in her. She knew her life depended on this scream, so she screamed with all the ferocity she could find against Edward. She just kept screaming and Edward looked at her as if he enjoyed watching her suffer. He was reaching down toward her pants again when suddenly he flew up and off her like a marionette with strings pulling him toward the ceiling.

Still clutching the poker, Edward was thrown back against the hearth, his lip cut by the gray stone as the edge of the poker landed in the fire's hot coals. He quickly recovered and looked up to see Jake towering over him.

Livi lay there in pain, her ribs either broken or severely bruised by Edward's poker prison. She watched as Jake's military strength was matched against Edward's insane adrenaline. The lunatic lunged at Jake with the poker and both men stood bobbing and weaving as if in the middle of some primitive native's dance.

"Well, look who's joined the party?" said Edward as he wiped the blood from his mouth.

"Put the poker down, Edward," Jake said.

"I don't take orders from some farm boy!" shouted Edward and he jabbed the white, hot poker tip toward Jake's stomach. Jake jumped back and realized he was in for a battle.

The men continued to bob and weave and lunge at each other, and in the middle of it all, the hot end of the poker somehow grazed Livi's antique curtains and they blazed up like parchment paper. The age of the home and its contents allowed the fire to spread quickly and Livi lay there, watching her home and planned memories burn around her.

The men were intent on each other and seemed oblivious to the fire so, amid the crackle of burning furniture, Livi just kept screaming, "Jake!" from the floor of her burning living room.

*

Jake heard Livi's screams behind him but he was too busy avoiding Edward's jabs to respond to her. Edward continued to swing the poker at Jake and actually caught skin a few times. Jake was fighting for both his life and Livi's, and he wished his opponent were at least somewhat sane.

He knew fighting a mad man was worse than fighting the best-trained sane enemy. Edward was unpredictable and Jake did not like that. Every time Jake thought he had Edward cornered, the lunatic would jab at him with the fire-breathing poker. Finally, Jake was able to make one solid punch meet Edward's jaw and his opponent fell. The killer's head crashed against the stone hearth and his blood poured into the fire's hot coals.

Jake quickly recovered out of fighting mode, and the flames surrounding him pulled him out of his small battlefield and into his next problem. He looked around and immediately realized the home's inevitable fate just as he spotted Livi still lying on the living room floor in front of the now smoking couch.

He scooped her up and ran through the front door and into the front yard. He gently placed Livi on the ground near his truck and raced back to the front porch. He heard Livi yelling for him as he reached the porch and realized there was nothing he could save. Flames escaped from every window and smoke drifted above the roof like a storm cloud. The entire home was already engulfed in fire and, if he tried to enter, he would be committing suicide in exchange for Livi's memories.

Chapter Twenty

It was a beautiful, crisp, clear fall afternoon and Livi sat in her front yard watching the remaining gray smoke drift up toward the few small white clouds decorating the blue sky. Her face and clothes were still smeared with soot, and the only clean thing she had on were the white bandages the paramedics wrapped around her broken ribs a few hours ago.

Gatsby sat at her side, still sleepy and wet from his nap in the backyard, and she reached over with much discomfort to give him a head rub, grateful for her furry miracle. The depths of her material losses had not reached her comprehension level yet, and she forcibly pushed thoughts of her mother's pictures and mementos to the back of her mind. It was too painful to think about what she had lost in the fire.

She heard a car drive up and slowly and excruciatingly turned to see Jake getting out of his truck.

"Hey," he said as he sat down beside her. He, too, was covered in grunge and smelled of ash.

"Hey." Livi tried to smile. "Is Todd finally finished with you?"

"Yeah. He finished taking my statement and said I was good to go. Edward's death was an accident and besides, he knows where to find me if he needs anything else." Jake looked over at the tear stains running through the soot on Livi's face. "How are you doing?" he asked as he tried to flash his trademark smile.

"Okay. How about you?" asked Livi softly.

"I guess I'm okay, too. Just a little dirty and banged up," said Jake as he surveyed what was left of Livi's house. "I am so very, very sorry about your home, Liv."

"I know. Me, too. But I think insurance will cover most of it," said Livi not wanting to mention the pictures and mementos she could never get back.

Jake must have heard the sadness in her voice because he quickly changed the subject. "They arrested Chamberlain. Todd said he and Edward were never going to pay out all that severance to the employees. They were just draining the money out of Hampton Steel so there would be nothing left. They hoped the company would close just like in New York. Do you know they had plans to disappear to the Caymans? They actually thought they could get away with it. How arrogant was that?" Jake paused then softly added, "Nadine really was going with them."

"I hate to hear that," Livi said. She missed her friend but could not believe she had been such a bad judge of her assistant's character.

Jake nodded, "Yeah. Todd said Mr. Sullivan is holding off closing Hampton Steel until he has time to look into this mess. He thinks they may be able to pull out the money Edward stashed in that fake account and put it back into Hampton Steel. You may have saved the company after all."

"Great," said Livi without much enthusiasm.

"Maybe you could get that big promotion now," said Jake, still trying hard to smile. "Todd said Joseph Sullivan is pulling Hampton Steel's strings now, and you know how much that old man loves you." Jake leaned over and gave her a slight nudge with his shoulder.

"Ouch," said Livi. Her injuries were going to take a while to heal.

"Oh, sorry! I forgot about your ribs," Jake said.

"That's okay. I'm fine, really," she said, rubbing her side. Livi had already decided she was not going back to Hampton Steel so her promotion had fallen off her life's radar. She did not know what she was going to do, she just knew that whatever it was, it would not be at Hampton Steel.

She did not mention this fact to Jake. She knew her work was a sore subject with him, and she was not in the mood for any heavy discussions right now. They sat in silence for a while, neither knowing what else to say.

"So, where are you and Gatsby going to stay?" Jake finally said.

"I don't know. Probably Dad's. He just left here with a boxful of a few things I was able to salvage from the fire," she responded. Livi knew she could always depend on her father. She and Jake continued to sit silently in her front yard, soaking in the warmth of the autumn sun, each lost in thought.

"Let's go for a ride," Jake said abruptly. He stood up and helped Livi slowly get on her feet.

"Where are we going?" Livi asked. She was not in the mood for guessing games.

"Do you have somewhere you have to be?" Jake asked sarcastically.

"No," Livi replied dejectedly.

"Then just get in the truck," Jake laughed. He was once again in caretaker mode.

He eased Livi into the truck, this time being extra cautious when he touched her, and soon the two of them, plus Gatsby, were riding through downtown Millersville. They drove past Nell's antique shop and Livi felt a lump in her throat as she remembered all the plans she had made for her now burned-out shell of a home. She looked over at the drooling mutt beside her and gave Gatsby another head rub to remind herself of what was truly important.

They soon arrived at the entrance to Jake's farm and the truck wound past the fields filled with horses and eventually stopped in front of the guesthouse.

"What are we doing here?" asked Livi.

"I want to show you something," said Jake as he flashed his mischievous smile at her. He slowly eased her out of the truck and helped her to the front door where Gatsby was already waiting. He opened the door wide for her and she entered the kitchen to find her unexpected surprise. There, hanging above the massive fireplace, was the Imari platter she had seen at Nell's that fateful day she had allowed Jake back into her life.

"My platter!" Livi squealed, "But how. . . why. . .?"

"I've had it for a while," Jake said. "I got it kind of hoping it would help make this place seem more like home. . . for you." Jake looked down at her with eyes so loving her butterflies were flitting around fast and furiously.

"Really?" said Livi batting her eyelashes.

"Really. If that is okay with you," he added.

"Absolutely." Livi smiled.

Jake leaned down and delicately kissed her. Livi kissed him back, finally content with herself and her place in this world. Her place was with Jake and she had at last realized Jake's soft kisses, and only his kisses, were the key to her happiness. She had spent all this time trying to control her life, to train her butterflies into submission, when, in reality, she never had any control of her life at all. In reality, her butterflies had actually been training *her* to be happy all this time.

Acknowledgments

Thank you, thank you, thank you to editor extraordinaire, Jennifer Lawler, who took a chance on an unknown aspiring author from Virginia. You truly do make dreams come true.

Thank you to Marilyn Naron, Moriah Densley, Jessica Verdi and all the other Ladies in Red at Crimson Romance. You are a kind and talented group who have taught me so much about this crazy publishing world.

Thank you to Tracie Blevins, Sue Carroll, Gina Davis and Betsy Sharrow who took the time to read, make suggestions and support my need to write. You are my forever friends who continually surprise me with your unconditional love.

Thank you to Lori Byington, my "sista" cousin and mistress of the English language. The hours, love and support you gave me and this book can never be repaid. Udooo!

Thank you to my family whose love reminds me that I already do have it all.

And most importantly, thank you to my husband and our two wonderful children for allowing me to disappear into the study each night and feed my need to write. You all are my life and the reason for my happiness. I am truly blessed.

Best wishes to all,
Lisa White

About the Author

Lisa White was born in Kingsport, Tennessee and raised in Bristol, Virginia. After graduating from the University of Virginia with a degree in Italian language and literature, she obtained her law degree from the University of Richmond School of Law. She currently lives in Southwest Virginia with her husband and two children. *The Laws of Love* is her first novel.

Please visit Lisa at: *www.lisawhiteauthor.com*

In the mood for more Crimson Romance? Check out *Caution: Filling Is Hot* by Tara Mills at CrimsonRomance.com.